BEYOND THE FARTHEST STAR

Also by
Edgar Rice Burroughs

TARZAN® SERIES
Tarzan of the Apes
The Return of Tarzan
The Beasts of Tarzan
The Son of Tarzan
Tarzan and the Jewels of Opar
Jungle Tales of Tarzan
Tarzan the Untamed
Tarzan the Terrible
Tarzan and the Golden Lion
Tarzan and the Ant Men
Tarzan, Lord of the Jungle
Tarzan and the Lost Empire
Tarzan at the Earth's Core
Tarzan the Invincible
Tarzan Triumphant
Tarzan and the City of Gold
Tarzan and the Lion Man
Tarzan and the Leopard Men
Tarzan's Quest
Tarzan the Magnificent
Tarzan and the Forbidden City
Tarzan and the Foreign Legion
Tarzan and the Madman
Tarzan and the Castaways
Tarzan and the Tarzan Twins
Tarzan: The Lost Adventure (with Joe R. Lansdale)

BARSOOM® SERIES
A Princess of Mars
The Gods of Mars
The Warlord of Mars
Thuvia, Maid of Mars
The Chessmen of Mars
The Master Mind of Mars
A Fighting Man of Mars
Swords of Mars
Synthetic Men of Mars
Llana of Gathol
John Carter of Mars

PELLUCIDAR® SERIES
At the Earth's Core
Pellucidar
Tanar of Pellucidar
Tarzan at the Earth's Core
Back to the Stone Age
Land of Terror
Savage Pellucidar

AMTOR™ SERIES
Pirates of Venus
Lost on Venus
Carson of Venus
Escape on Venus
The Wizard of Venus

Caspak™ Series
The Land That Time Forgot
The People That Time Forgot
Out of Time's Abyss

Va-nah™ Series
The Moon Maid
The Moon Men
The Red Hawk

The Mucker™ Series
The Mucker
The Return of the Mucker
The Oakdale Affair

The Custers™ Series
The Eternal Savage
The Mad King

The Apache Series
The War Chief
Apache Devil

Western Tales
The Bandit of Hell's Bend
The Deputy Sheriff of
Comanche County

Historical Tales
The Outlaw of Torn
I Am a Barbarian

Parallel Worlds
Beyond Thirty
Minidoka: 937th Earl of
One Mile Series M

Other Tales
The Cave Girl
The Monster Men
The Man-Eater

The Girl from Farris's
The Lad and the Lion
The Rider
The Efficiency Expert
The Girl from Hollywood
Jungle Girl
Beware!/The Scientists Revolt
Pirate Blood
Marcia of the Doorstep
You Lucky Girl!
Forgotten Tales of Love
and Murder

ERBurroughs.com

Restored Edition

EDGAR RICE BURROUGHS

COVER ART BY
FRANK FRAZETTA

FRONTISPIECE BY
MARK SCHULTZ

ILLUSTRATIONS BY
ROY G. KRENKEL

PREFACE BY
CHRISTOPHER PAUL CAREY

INTRODUCTION BY
PAUL DI FILIPPO

EDGAR RICE BURROUGHS, INC.
PUBLISHERS
TARZANA   CALIFORNIA

BEYOND THE FARTHEST STAR
© 1941, 1964, 2021 Edgar Rice Burroughs, Inc.

This special Restored Edition compilation and all other new material therein © 2021 Edgar Rice Burroughs, Inc.

Frontispiece by Mark Schultz, preface, and introduction © 2021 Edgar Rice Burroughs, Inc.

Cover art by Frank Frazetta, illustrations by Roy G. Krenkel, maps of Poloda and the Planetary System of Omos, and Unisan Alphabet and Numbers © 1964 Edgar Rice Burroughs, Inc.

All rights reserved. Except as otherwise permitted by law, no part of this book may be reproduced, stored in a retrieval system, or transmitted in any form or by any means, electronic, mechanical, photocopying, recording or otherwise, without the written permission of the publisher, except for brief passages quoted in a review.

Trademarks Beyond the Farthest Star™, Tarzan®, Tarzan of the Apes®, Lord of the Jungle®, Barsoom®, Pellucidar®, Carson of Venus®, Amtor™, The Land That Time Forgot®, Caspak®, Va-nah™, The Mucker™, The Custers™, Victory Harben™, and Edgar Rice Burroughs® owned by Edgar Rice Burroughs, Inc. Associated logos (including the Doodad symbol; ERB, Inc., solar system colophon; Beyond the Farthest Star logo; and Omos Star System logo), characters, names, and the distinctive likenesses thereof are trademarks or registered trademarks of Edgar Rice Burroughs, Inc.

Special thanks to Jason Scott Aiken, Christopher Paul Carey, Paul Di Filippo, Henry G. Franke III, Bill Hillman, Janet Mann, Mark Schultz, James Sullos, Jess Terrell, Michael Tierney, Cathy Wilbanks, Charlotte Wilbanks, and Mike Wolfer for their valuable assistance in producing this book.

Published by Edgar Rice Burroughs, Inc.
Tarzana, California
EdgarRiceBurroughs.com

ISBN-13: 978-1-945462-36-8

- 9 8 7 6 5 4 3 2 1 -

TABLE OF CONTENTS

Maps ix
Unisan Alphabet and Numbers xi
Preface by Christopher Paul Carey. xiii
Introduction by Paul Di Filippo. xix

PART I:
ADVENTURE ON POLODA

Chapter	Page
Foreword	.1
Chapter One	.3
Chapter Two	.9
Chapter Three	14
Chapter Four	18
Chapter Five	22
Chapter Six	27
Chapter Seven	35
Chapter Eight	39
Chapter Nine	45
Chapter Ten	51
Chapter Eleven	56
Chapter Twelve	63
Chapter Thirteen	69

PART II:
TANGOR RETURNS

Foreword 77
Chapter One 79
Chapter Two 86

CHAPTER THREE.	. 93
CHAPTER FOUR	100
CHAPTER FIVE	106
CHAPTER SIX	113
CHAPTER SEVEN	119
CHAPTER EIGHT	124
CHAPTER NINE	130
CHAPTER TEN	137
BONUS MATERIALS.	145
EDGAR RICE BURROUGHS: MASTER OF ADVENTURE	179
ABOUT THE ARTISTS	180
ABOUT EDGAR RICE BURROUGHS, INC.	181

PLANETARY SYSTEM OF OMOS
FROM THE DIRECTION OF EARTH, LOCATED APPROXIMATELY TWENTY-TWO THOUSAND LIGHT-YEARS BEYOND GLOBULAR CLUSTER NGC 7006

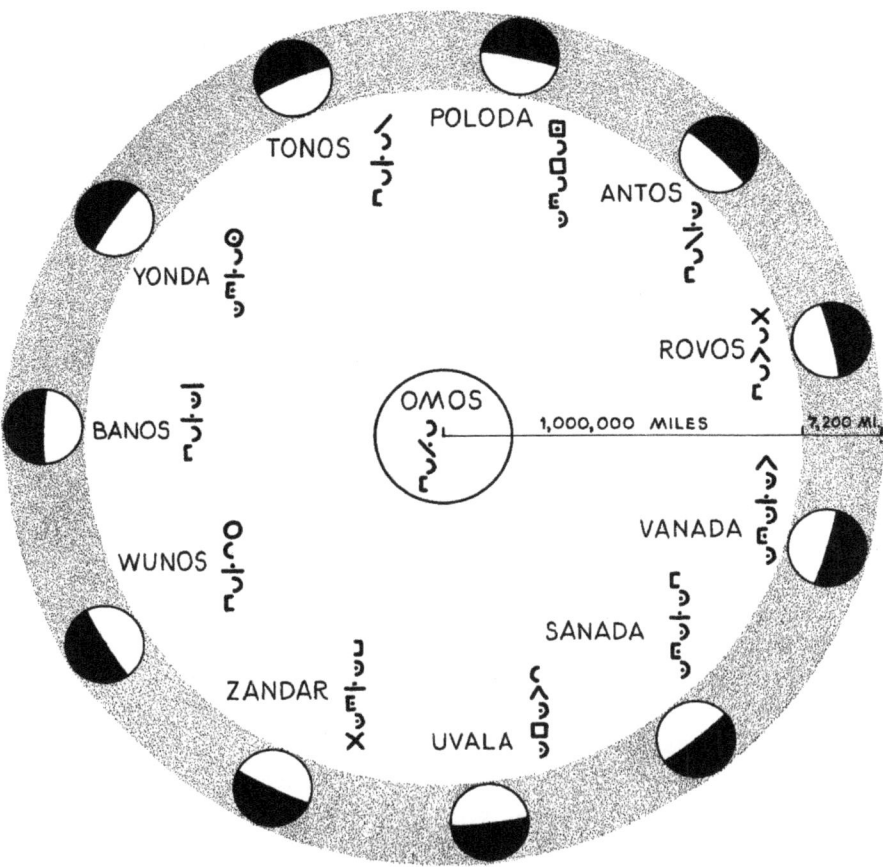

The names of the star Omos and each of its planets are given in the Unisan language and their English equivalents.

POLODA

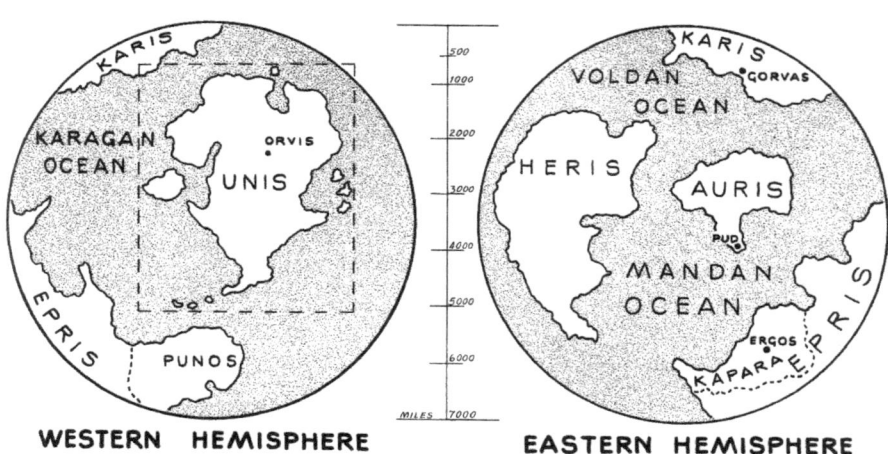

WESTERN HEMISPHERE   EASTERN HEMISPHERE

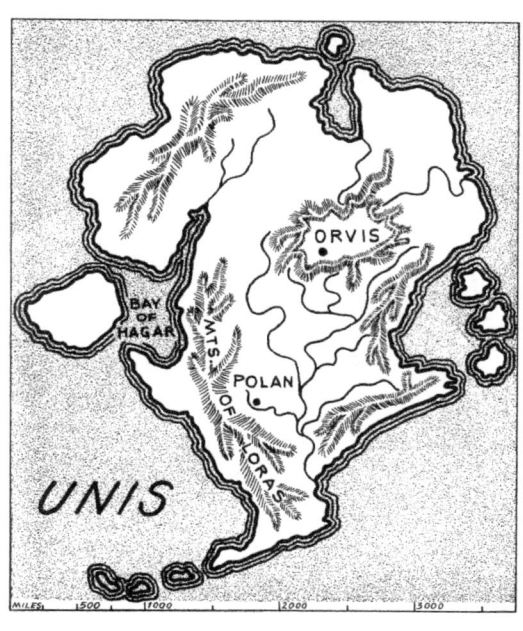

UNISAN ALPHABET AND NUMBERS

C	USA	U	Ǝ	HUL	H	⊥	DOT	0
⊃	OM	O	□	LUH	L	|	AL	1
⊂	ETA	E	⊡	PAN	P	⊤	VAN	2
⊋	AVA	A	/	TAM	T	⊥	SOO	3
✕	ILA	I	\	FUH	F	⊻	LO	4
O	WUH	W	⁄	JU	J	φ	TAN	5
⊙	YAK	Y	⟍	MI	M	φ	HUV	6
—	BOS	B	✕	RUH	R	Ⅱ	JAN	7
o—	GAR	G	∧	VIK	V	Ⅹ	BOR	8
⁼	KOB	K	∨	SHA	CH	Ⅲ	KO	9
⁺	NUH	N	∧	ANG	NG	⊥	ALDOT	10
⊏	SKO	S	=		COMMA	⫯	ALAL	11
⊐	ZUH	Z	≡		PERIOD	⊤	ALVAN	12
E	DAR	D	✓		QUESTION	⊥	ALSOO	13

THERE IS NO C, Q, OR X.

⊋	□	/	/	⊡	/	⊡	Ǝ	/
✕	✕	⊃	Ǝ	⊃	⊃	⊃	C	C
		∧	C	□	⊥	⊥	∧	≡
		⊃		⊃		∧	⊃	
		⊏		E		E		
				⊃		✕		
						∧		
						⊃		
						⊥		

⊤	VANDOT	20
⊤	VANAL	21
⊥	SOODOT	30
⊻	LODOT	40
φ	TANDOT	50
⊥	ALDOTDOT	100

TRANSLATION:
ARA LI TOVOS THU POLODA TAN PANDARVAN HUVO TU.
ON THE PLANET OF POLODA FIVE CONTINENTS THERE ARE.

PREFACE
A CLASSIC SF NOVEL RESTORED
CHRISTOPHER PAUL CAREY

IT IS IRONIC, prescient, and at the same time not terribly surprising that Edgar Rice Burroughs wrote in his foreword to the present novel that he could not guarantee the story would reach the reader exactly as it was typed; this, he proclaimed, was because "it must pass through the hands of editors, and an editor would edit the word of God." Even more ironically, that very sentence from his foreword did not escape the editor's red pen. Knowing the author's wry sense of humor, I almost wonder if he laid down his decree as an irresistible trap for the unsuspecting editor, so that he might exclaim, "You see—I was right!"

Even as Burroughs rose to fame and became one of the most popular writers of the twentieth century, he looked on as various editors of the pulp magazines, in which his stories typically first appeared, tweaked his prose or even substantially rewrote it and cut passages. Sometimes these emendations and excisions may have occurred because of such practical considerations as the constraints of layout or the desired length of the periodical, but other times it was certainly due to the whim of the individual editor. Soon, the author undertook the frequent practice of restoring the text from his original manuscripts when his stories were subsequently published in book form. But it is an oversimplification to maintain this was always the case.

In one rare instance, for example, when *The Moon Maid* was being prepared for publication by A. C. McClurg, Burroughs himself took a buzz saw to his own work, cutting approximately fifteen thousand words because of the publisher's wish for a reduced page count. After all, Burroughs was both a practical and an astute businessman, and he did what he had to if it meant he could sell another story and continue to build on his highly successful career.

The first installment of *Beyond the Farthest Star*, appearing herein as "Part I: Adventure on Poloda," was first published in the January 1942 issue of *Blue Book* magazine. "Part II: Tangor Returns," however, did not see print until the 1964 Canaveral Press hardcover collection *Tales of Three Planets*, where it appeared alongside Part I some fourteen years after the author's death. For this reason, Burroughs never got his chance to restore the text of his original manuscript for the hardcover publication—and there *were* a number of significant changes to Part I made by the editor at *Blue Book*. Correspondence indicates that Edgar Rice Burroughs' secretary, Cyril Ralph Rothmund, submitted the novella to *Blue Book* editor Donald Kennicott, who purchased it, but no letters could be located indicating a discussion of changes made to the story or the identity of the editor who implemented them. As Rothmund handled all business matters related to the story, it would appear likely that the editorial changes were made without consulting the author.

No real substantive changes were made when Richard A. Lupoff edited Part II for Canaveral, beyond the curious omission of a line of dialogue in Chapter Ten ("'Get out!' he growled.") and the adjective "scowling" from the previous sentence. These exclusions only serve to make the scene somewhat confusing, and therefore may have been simply accidental transcription errors.

All subsequent English-language editions of *Beyond the Farthest Star* to date appear to have been based on the

Canaveral Press text, Part I of which follows the *Blue Book* text. Therefore, until the present Restored Edition, readers have been denied the pleasure of experiencing the novel as Edgar Rice Burroughs intended.

There are many reasons, both idiosyncratic and justified, why an editor may alter or cut an author's words. So what exactly happened with the pulp magazine text? Examining the historical context in which Edgar Rice Burroughs wrote the novel may shed some light on the matter.

The author's meticulous recordkeeping indicates that he wrote Part I (which appeared in *Blue Book* under the title "Beyond the Farthest Star") from October 24 to November 5, 1940. Part II, "Tangor Returns," was written in a similarly furious span of productivity, from December 17 to December 21, 1940. At this time, the world was plunging into the darkness of war. Poland and France had fallen to the Nazis; the Battle of Britain had just been waged; the Blitz was underway as the German *Luftwaffe* continued to lead nighttime bombing raids over the United Kingdom; and, like falling dominos, Hungary, Romania, Bulgaria, and the Slovak Republic had all just signed on to the Tripartite Pact with the Axis Powers.

Against this bleak and distressing backdrop, Burroughs decided to write a science fiction adventure distinctly darker and grittier than his typical Tarzan or John Carter fare. The city of Orvis in his new story, with its buildings that retreat into the ground to escape destruction from the continuous aerial bombing raids of the enemy Kapars, is no gleaming, utopian metropolis like Greater and Lesser Helium from the Barsoom stories. The mantra "It is war" echoes throughout *Beyond the Farthest Star*, a far cry from John Carter's motto, "I still live!" And although there is a hint of a budding romance between the protagonist—Tangor—and a young woman in the novel, a relationship the author may have developed had he written the story in his usual four parts instead of just two, this never comes to fruition, thus causing the tale to depart even further from Burroughs' literary hallmarks.

Beyond changes made to the author's punctuation (edits that sometimes made a sentence less clear or more grammatically dubious than the original) and a number of excised lines and phrases throughout, the most significant and lengthiest passages that were cut related to the stark realities and grim horrors of war. Here likely lies the answer to why such edits were made. As it became clear that the United States was falling headlong into the global conflict, it would have been demoralizing to the readership for the story to go into detail, for example, about how the bodies of the war dead of the nation of Unis (clearly a stand-in for the "United States") are processed as food by the enemy so that they might feed their war-ravaged, subjugated peoples, as stated in one excised passage. At another point in the story Harkas Don, the son of the family that adopts and acculturates the alien Tangor, is envious of Tangor and Bantor Han's experiences hunting in the mountains. Harkas Don never had the opportunity to indulge in such a sport because citizens of Unis, from age fifteen until they are too old to fight, have only one day off from the war effort in every ten. The excised passage concludes by explaining how the retired soldiers "go quietly out of the city, and are seen no more," and how "they pine for quiet, and rest, and peace; and from the moment that they are born the only place that they can hope to find it is in a grave." These are certainly not morale-boosting sentiments for a nation gearing up for war!

Other portions were apparently trimmed from the first part of the novel at the editor's caprice. These include Tangor's fear that, despite his resurrection on the planet Poloda, he could die a very real mortal death there, as well as foreshadowing about the technology needed for interplanetary travel that would go on to feature in Part II. The author's dryly humorous, but entertaining, characterization of the soldier Bantor Han as a hopeless pessimist was similarly cut. And a mention of contemporary crime gangs back on Earth was also removed, along with "Hague of New Jersey," a reference to Frank Hague, a prominent politician of the day, whose desk was said to have been equipped with a secret drawer through which lobbyists could pass him bribes. Moreover, the editor at *Blue Book* combined chapters from the manuscript, creating eleven instead of the original thirteen, thereby subtly changing the dramatic flow of the story from the author's intention.

These and other alterations have been reversed in the present edition of the novel, and the text of Edgar Rice Burroughs' original manuscript has been restored, making this the first definitive version of *Beyond the Farthest Star* ever published. This historic edition of the novel is long overdue, and releasing it now couldn't be better timed, as the Omos star system is now being actively explored in the expanding series of Edgar Rice Burroughs Universe literature and comic books. Beyond Poloda lie ten more planets in the system waiting to tell their tales of adventure—each connected by an atmosphere belt that allows for easy travel between them via airplane.

Before closing out this preface, I feel it is relevant to mention that one of the alternative titles for *Beyond the Farthest Star* was *The Ghostly Script*. Those more studied in Burroughs' work will recognize the title as the same he had given to an unpublished novel that he began writing in March 1920, then abandoned for a decade before resuming it again in October 1930, and ultimately left unfinished at approximately 7,000 words in length. Just as in *Beyond the Farthest Star*, the narrative of *The Ghostly Script* was related to Burroughs by means of spectral fingers clacking out the story on his typewriter as he rolled blank page after blank page onto the platen. It is one of his most unusual tales, featuring the protagonist John Lee, a Black sergeant who died at the Battle of San Juan Hill during the Spanish–American War and woke up in the afterlife upon a strange world with three suns, which occupies the same space as our Earth but is located at a different "angle."

When I first read the unpublished manuscript, it occurred to me that *The Ghostly Script*, even in its unfinished state, provides a sort of skeleton key to unlocking some of the deepest mysteries of the ERB Universe, whereby Burroughs sought to elucidate a coherent framework to connect the far-flung worlds of his fantastical tales. Namely, it hints at the "science" behind how such characters as John Carter and Ulysses Paxton from the Barsoom series, Betty Callwell from the Amtor series, and Tangor from *Beyond the Farthest Star* effected their interplanetary travel.

It is interesting that in *Beyond the Farthest Star*, Tangor relates his narrative to Burroughs more or less as events are unfolding in the present from the viewpoint of our hero, and yet never does the reader learn the story behind how Tangor discovered the means of spirit communication. It may be that one day the aforementioned skeleton key will turn in the tumbler of this mystery, as well, and begin to unlock answers in new tales expanding the canon of the ERB Universe. And perhaps that key is already turning....

CHRISTOPHER PAUL CAREY *is the Director of Publishing and Creative Director of the ERB Universe at Edgar Rice Burroughs, Inc. He is the author of* Swords Against the Moon Men—*an authorized sequel to Edgar Rice Burroughs' classic science fantasy novel* The Moon Maid—*and the ERB Universe novel* Victory Harben: Fires of Halos. *He has scripted several comic books set in Mr. Burroughs' worlds, including* Pellucidar: Across Savage Seas, Pellucidar: Dark of the Sun, *and* Carson of Venus: The Flames Beyond. *He has edited more than sixty novels, anthologies, and collections for a variety of publishers, and had the honor of working with Mr. Burroughs' original manuscript to prepare the text for the present edition of* Beyond the Farthest Star. *He lives in Southern California.*

INTRODUCTION
(MULTIPLE) LIVES DURING WARTIME
PAUL DI FILIPPO

ANY READERS WHO BELIEVE they have Edgar Rice Burroughs completely and simplistically sussed out, and are confident that they can predict exactly what his fiction sounds like, and how he might treat any particular theme or topic or set of characters, are directed henceforth and immediately to a close study of *Beyond the Farthest Star*, herewith reprinted in a singularly expanded edition with much valuable ancillary material. This short novel—really two novellas of identical vintage, yet with an intriguing publishing history marked by a large interregnum—shows Burroughs working in fresh, surprising, deeply affecting territory vastly different from his two most famous franchises, the undying realms of John Carter and Tarzan. Although certain authorial similarities do obtain across Burroughs' whole canon, the feel, import, and lineage of *Beyond the Farthest Star* lies laterally abaft the more well-known mythoi.

Before taking a look at the literary qualities and characteristics of *Beyond the Farthest Star*, it might be useful to very, very briefly attempt to summarize the charms and atmosphere of John Carter and Tarzan, so as to recognize the baseline from which *Beyond the Farthest Star* is deviating.

The first books in both series, *A Princess of Mars* and *Tarzan of the Apes*, both published in magazine form in

1912, hail from the Belle Époque, that brief and glorious era distinguished, so Wikipedia tells us, "by optimism, regional peace, economic prosperity, colonial expansion, and technological, scientific, and cultural innovations." The books predate the full flowering of Hollywood and the cinema, and partake of older, more theatrical forms of staged entertainment, being more congenial to melodrama as opposed to naturalism. Their language is more ornate, a style still finding a path between Victorian locutions and the twentieth-century demotic. The heroes shared more in common with classical figures like Hercules and Beowulf than they did with the modern protagonists just around the bend of time, as-yet-unborn personages from Hemingway and Fitzgerald, Faulkner and Dos Passos. And the women too derived more from ancient icons of purity, frontier fierceness and allure, admixed with Belle Époque virtues of modesty, daintiness and spousal loyalty.

A quirk of mine is that I mentally associate both John Carter and Tarzan with *The Music Man*, a drama written of course much later, but also set in 1912. Reading the books evokes for me that mid-century simulation. I can easily picture either of Burroughs' stalwart heroes, suitably spiffed up, walking the streets of River City and vying for the affections of Marian the Librarian.

Most importantly, both books were composed prior to that grim titanic milestone, World War I. As such, they reflect the prelapsarian innocence which that first global conflagration would forever destroy. And because several of the sequels in each franchise were also written before the war, all these attributes I've cited were firmly cemented into place, even continuing onward, in those volumes written post-1918.

Now consider *Beyond the Farthest Star*, written not when Edgar Rice Burroughs was a hopeful spring chicken of thirty-seven, but when he was a publishing-hardened, life-tempered sixty-five, fully embarked on his senior years.

It would seem psychologically unnatural indeed if Burroughs were able, when embarking on a brand-new project whose template and personality were not already set in stone by marketplace and audience demands, to recreate the same attitude and themes as in his earlier works. But more importantly, the surrounding world at large circa 1940–41 was the largest determinant of the new series. Its creation mirrored the times and reflected Burroughs' worries and preoccupations. Although not yet involved officially in the war, the USA was caught up peripherally in the global turmoil, and any citizen who read the news from abroad could gauge the horrors in play and anticipate the nation's future involvement.

And so we come to the saga of Tangor, an Earthman who dies most incontestably—bullet through the heart—while fighting an aerial battle with the Germans, and awakes to find himself on the planet Poloda in the Omos system, nearly half a million light-years from our Solar System. (This expanded cosmic scope surely owes much to Burroughs' appreciation of all the scientific findings and new understandings that had occurred since the composition of *A Princess of Mars*. And the construction of the Omos system, with its belt of co-orbital worlds, researched with the help of a professional astronomer, speaks to Burroughs' desire to utilize new discoveries.)

But Poloda is no Barsoom, replete with colorful and exotic civilizations and princesses and swordplay and feats of brawny derring-do, nor is it the unspoiled realm of darkest Africa (although we will see a bit of Poloda's wilderness and beasts). Rendered in very stark and plain language, it is a world of perpetual warfare involving machines—mainly planes with bombs. Honorable hand-to-hand combat is replaced by killing the enemy in the hundreds and thousands from high above, and even the Red Baron–style dogfights with unseen opponents lack glory or zest.

The country that Tangor adopts—Unis—is admirable and noble, but constricted mentally and culturally by the ceaseless hostilities of decades. Tangor recognized and regrets this stultification. Fighters are almost interchangeable cogs of the war apparatus, not a single heroic and irascible Tars Tarkas among them. Tangor finds this hard to stomach, and of course, as a scion of alien values and virtues, comes to stand out from these commodified figures.

The women likewise are admirable, but thoroughly mundane and practical—when they are not vile sleazy traitors like Morga Sagra. No sparks of love are ignited between Tangor and his hostess, Harkas Yamoda, just friendship and respect as allies in a righteous cause.

Tangor's exploits in the first half of the novel are suitably stirring in a standard battlefield Purple Heart manner, albeit far from legendary, and he acquits himself strongly. He does indeed share some of the genes of his earlier cousins, John Carter and Tarzan. But it is in the second half of the book—written coevally with the first part, but not published until long after Burroughs' death—that our author achieves his triumph, rendering this book so different and such a valuable part of his canon. Tangor must go undercover into the enemy land of the Kapars to bring back their technological invention that could break the stalemate of the conflict—as well as open up the Omos system to interplanetary exploration.

Burroughs' chilling portrait of the totalitarian Kapar state is unrelenting and grimly, granularly precise. Modeled on both Nazi Germany and Stalin's USSR, Kapar proleptically evokes all the mid-century dystopias just over the horizon, from *1984* to *Brave New World*, from Philip K. Dick's *The Penultimate Truth* (where underground cities definitely echo those of Poloda), down to *THX 1138* and Hugh Howey's Wool series. I would not be surprised if Burroughs had encountered Zamyatin's *We* (1924) and used it as an inspiration. Lastly, thanks to the espionage-in-a-dictatorship motif, I see prefigurations here of Cordwainer Smith's *Atomsk*, from a few years later in 1949.

At one point the mother of Harkas Yamoda gives vent to some uncommon rage:

> "Planes!" said Yamoda's mother bitterly. "Planes! The curse of the world. History tells us that when they were first perfected and men first flew in the air over Poloda, there was great rejoicing, and the men who perfected them were heaped with honors. They were to bring the peoples of the world closer together. They were to break down international barriers of fear and suspicion. They were to revolutionize society by bringing all peoples together, to make a better and happier world in which to live. Through them civilization was to be advanced hundreds of years; and what have they done? They have blasted civilization from nine-tenths of Poloda and stopped its advance in the other tenth. They have destroyed a hundred thousand cities and millions of people, and they have driven those who have survived underground, to live the lives of burrowing rodents. Planes! The curse of all times. I hate them. They have taken thirteen of my sons, and now they have taken my daughter."

The reverence for planes that the grieving mother curses is plainly the same naively optimistic vision of a technocratic elite bringing peace to the planet that H. G. Wells expressed in his conception of "Wings Over the World" in *Things to Come* (1936). In this indictment, Burroughs has thus chosen to level his big guns against the very same forces of "progress" that had destroyed the Belle Époque and threatened to turn Tarzan and John Carter, despite their universal appeal, into anachronisms on the verge of extinction. Burroughs at age sixty-five tossed out a lifeline—or at least a screed of passionate defiance—back to the Burroughs of age thirty-seven, letting his earlier avatar and the rest of us know that better worlds should not die wholly unlamented.

PAUL DI FILIPPO *sold his first story in 1977, and since then has produced over forty books of short and novel-length fiction. He lives in Providence, Rhode Island, where he haunts H. P. Lovecraft's footsteps daily, with his partner Deborah Newton and a cocker spaniel named Moxie.*

BEYOND THE FARTHEST STAR

PART I

ADVENTURE ON POLODA

FOREWORD

WE HAD ATTENDED a party at Diamond Head; and after dinner, comfortable on hikiee and easy chair on the lanai, we fell to talking about the legends and superstitions of the ancient Hawaiians.

There were a number of old-timers there, several with a mixture of Hawaiian and American blood, and we were the only malihinis—happy to be there, and happy to listen.

Most Hawaiian legends are rather childish, though often amusing; but many of their superstitions are grim and sinister—and they are not confined to ancient Hawaiians either. You couldn't get a modern kane or wahine with a drop of Hawaiian blood in his veins to touch the bones or relics still often found in hidden burial caves in the mountains, nor many haole kamaainas either, for that matter. They seem to feel the same way about kahunas, and that it is just as easy to be polite to a kahuna as not—and much safer.

I am not superstitious, and I don't believe in ghosts; so what I heard that evening didn't have any other effect on me than to entertain me. It couldn't have been connected in any way with what happened later that night, for I scarcely gave it a thought after we left the home of our friends; and I really don't know why I have mentioned it at all, except that it has to do with strange happenings; and what happened later that night certainly falls into that category.

We had come home quite early; and I was in bed by eleven o'clock, but I couldn't sleep; so I got up about midnight, thinking I would work a little on the outline of a new story I had in mind.

I sat in front of my typewriter just staring at the keyboard, trying to recall a vagrant idea that I had thought pretty clever at the time, but which now eluded me. I stared so long and so steadily that the keys commenced to blur and run together.

A nice white sheet of paper peeped shyly out from the underneath side of the platen, a virgin sheet of paper as yet undefiled by the hand of man. My hands were clasped over that portion of my anatomy where I once had a waistline; they were several inches from the keyboard when the thing happened—the keys commenced to depress themselves with bewildering rapidity, and one neat line of type after another appeared upon that virgin paper, still undefiled by the hand of man; but who was defiling it? Or what?

I blinked my eyes and shook my head, convinced that I had fallen asleep at the typewriter; but I hadn't—somebody, or something, was typing a message there and typing it faster than any human hands ever typed.

I am passing it on just as I first saw it, but I can't guarantee that it will come to you just as it was typed that night—it must pass through the hands of editors, and an editor would edit the word of God.

CHAPTER ONE

I WAS SHOT DOWN behind the German lines in September 1939. Three Messerschmitts had attacked me, but I had the satisfaction of seeing two of them spinning down to earth, whirling funeral pyres, before I took the last long dive.

My name is—well, never mind; my family still retains many of the Puritanical characteristics of our revered ancestors, and it is so publicity shy that it would consider a death notice as verging on the vulgar. My family thinks that I am dead; so let it go at that—perhaps I am. I imagine the Germans buried me, anyway.

The transition, or whatever it was, must have been instantaneous; for my head was still whirling from the spin when I opened my eyes in what appeared to be a garden. There were trees and shrubs and flowers and expanses of well-kept lawn; but what astonished me first was that there didn't seem to be any end to the garden—it just extended indefinitely all the way to the horizon, or at least as far as I could see—and there were no buildings nor any people.

At least I didn't see any people at first; and I was mighty glad of that, because I didn't have on any clothes. I thought I must be dead—I knew I must after what I had been through. When a machine-gun bullet lodges in your heart, you remain conscious for about fifteen seconds—long enough to realize that you have already gone into your last spin—but you still know you are dead, unless a miracle has happened to save you. I thought that possibly such a miracle might have intervened to preserve me for posterity.

I looked around for the Germans and for my plane, but they weren't there; then, for the first time, I noticed the trees and shrubs and flowers in more detail, and I realized that I had never seen anything like them. They were not astoundingly different from those with which I had been familiar, but they were of species I had never seen nor noticed. It then occurred to me that I had fallen into a German botanical garden.

It also occurred to me that it might be a good plan to ascertain if I were badly injured. I had no pain, but that didn't necessarily prove anything. I tried to stand, and I succeeded; and I was just congratulating myself on having escaped so miraculously, when I heard a feminine scream.

I wheeled about to face a girl looking at me in open-eyed astonishment, with just a tinge of terror. The moment I turned, she did likewise and fled. So did I; I fled to the concealment of a clump of bushes.

And then I commenced to wonder. I had never seen a girl exactly like her before, nor one garbed as was she. If it hadn't been broad daylight, I would have thought she might be going to a fancy dress ball. Her body had been sheathed in what appeared to be gold sequins; and she looked as though she had either been poured into her costume, or it had been pasted on her bare skin. It was undeniably a good fit. From the yoke to a pair of red boots that flapped about her ankles and halfway to her knees, she had been clothed in sequins.

Her skin was the whitest I had ever seen on any human being, while her hair was an indescribable copper-colored titian. I hadn't had a really good look at her features; and I really couldn't say that she was beautiful, but just the glimpse that I had had assured me that she was no Gorgon.

After I had concealed myself in the shrubbery, I looked to see what had become of the girl; but she was nowhere to be seen. What had become of her? Where had she gone? She had simply disappeared.

All about this vast garden were mounds of earth upon which trees and shrubbery grew. They were not very high, perhaps six feet; and the trees and shrubbery planted around them so blended into the growth upon them that they were scarcely noticeable; but directly in front of me, I noticed an opening in one of them; and as I was looking at it, five men came out of it, like rabbits out of a warren.

They were all dressed alike—in red sequins with black boots—and on their heads were large metal helmets beneath which I could see locks of yellow hair. Their skin was very white, too, like the girl's. They wore swords and were carrying enormous pistols, not quite as large as Tommy guns, but nonetheless formidable-looking.

They seemed to be looking for someone! I had a vague suspicion that they were looking for me—well, it wasn't such a vague suspicion after all.

After having seen the beautiful garden and the girl, I might have thought that, having been killed, I was in Heaven; but after seeing these men garbed in red, and recalling some of the things I had done in my past life, I decided that I had probably gone to the other place.

I was pretty well concealed; but I could watch everything they did; and when, pistols in hand, they commenced a systematic search of the shrubbery, I knew that they were looking for me and that they would find me; so I stepped out into the open.

At sight of me, they surrounded me, and one of them commenced to fire words at me in a language that might have been a Japanese broadcast combined with a symphony concert.

"Am I dead?" I asked.

They looked at one another; and then they spoke to me again; but I couldn't understand a syllable, much less a word, of what they said. Finally one of them came up and took me by the arm; and the others surrounded us, and they started to lead me away. Then it was that I saw the most amazing thing I have ever seen in my life: Out of that vast garden rose buildings! They came up swiftly all around us—buildings of all sizes and shapes, but all trim and streamlined, and extremely beautiful in their simplicity; and on top of them they carried the trees and the shrubbery beneath which they had been concealed.

"Where am I?" I demanded. "Can't any of you speak English, or French, or German, or Spanish, or Italian?"

They looked at me blankly, and spoke to one another in that language that did not sound like a language at all. They took me into one of the buildings that had grown out of the garden. It was full of people, both men and women; and they were all dressed in skin-tight clothing. They looked at me in amazement and amusement and disgust; and some of the women tittered and covered their eyes with their hands; but at last one of my escort found a robe and covered me, and I felt very much better. You have no idea what it does to one's ego to find oneself in the nude among a multitude of people; and as I realized my predicament, I commenced to laugh. My captors looked at me in astonishment; they didn't know that I had suddenly realized that I was the victim of a bad dream: I had not flown over Germany; I had not been shot down; I had never been in a garden with a strange girl—I was just dreaming.

"Run along," I said, "you are just a bad dream—beat it!" And then I said "Boo!" at them, thinking that that would wake me up; but it didn't. It only made a couple of them seize me by either arm and hustle me along to a room where there was an elderly man seated at

"Out of that vast garden rose buildings!"

a desk. He wore a skin-tight suit of black spangles with white boots.

My captors spoke to the man at length. He looked at me and shook his head; then he said something to them; and they took me into an adjoining room where there was a cage, and they put me in the cage and chained me to one of the bars.

CHAPTER TWO

I WILL NOT bore you with what happened during the ensuing six weeks; suffice it to say that I learned a lot from Harkas Yen, the elderly man into whose keeping I had been placed. I learned, for instance, that he is a psychiatrist, and that I had been placed in his hands for observation. When the girl who had screamed had reported me, and the police had come and arrested me, they had all thought that I was a lunatic.

Harkas Yen taught me the language; and I learned it quickly, because I have always been something of a linguist. As a child, I traveled much in Europe, going to schools in France, Italy, and Germany, while my father was the military attaché at those legations; and so I imagine I developed an aptitude for languages.

He questioned me most carefully when he discovered that the language I spoke was wholly unknown in his world, and eventually he came to believe the strange story I told him of my transition from my own world to his.

I do not believe in transmigration, reincarnation or metempsychosis; and neither did Harkas Yen, but we found it very difficult to adjust our beliefs to the obvious facts of my case. I had been on Earth, a planet of which Harkas Yen had not the slightest knowledge; and now I was on Poloda, a planet of which I had never heard. I spoke a language that no man on Poloda had ever heard, and I could not understand one word of the five principal languages of Poloda.

After a few weeks Harkas Yen took me out of the cage and put me up in his own home. He obtained for me a brown sequin suit and a pair of brown boots; and I had the run of his house; but I was not permitted to leave it, either while it was sunk belowground or while it was raised to the surface.

That house went up and down at least once a day, and sometimes oftener. I could tell when it was going down by the screaming of sirens, and I could tell why it was down by the detonation of bursting bombs that shook everything in the place and would have demolished it had it remained on the surface.

I asked Harkas Yen what it was all about, although I could pretty well guess by what I had left in the making on Earth; but all he said was: "The Kapars."

After I had learned the language so that I could speak and understand it, Harkas Yen announced that I was to be tried.

"For what?" I asked.

"Well, Tangor," he replied, "I guess it is to discover whether you are a spy, a lunatic, or a dangerous character who should be destroyed for the good of Unis."

Tangor was the name he had given me. It means *from nothing*, and he said that it quite satisfactorily described my origin; because from my own testimony I came from a planet which did not exist. Unis is the name of the country to which I had been so miraculously transported. It was not Heaven and it was certainly not Hell, except when the Kapars came over with their bombs.

At my trial there were three judges and an audience; the only witnesses were the girl who had discovered me; the five policemen who had arrested me; Harkas Yen; his son, Harkas Don; his daughter, Harkas Yamoda; and his wife. At least I thought that those were all the witnesses, but I was mistaken. There were seven more, old gentlemen with sparse gray hairs on their chins—you've got to be an old man on Poloda before you can raise a beard, and even then it is nothing to brag about.

The judges were fine-looking men in gray sequin suits and gray boots; they were very dignified. Like all the judges in Unis, they are appointed by the government for life, on the recommendation of what corresponds to a bar association in America. They can be impeached, but otherwise they hold office until they are seventy years old, when they can be reappointed if they are again recommended by the association of lawyers.

The session opened with a simple little ritual; everyone rose when the judges entered the courtroom; and after they had taken their places, every one, including the judges, said, "For the honor and glory of Unis," in unison; then I was conducted to the prisoner's dock, I guess you would call it; and one of the judges asked me my name.

"I am called Tangor," I replied.

"From what country do you come?"

"From the United States of America."

"Where is that?"

"On the planet Earth."

"Where is that?"

"Now you have me stumped," I said. "If I were on Mercury, Venus, Mars, or any other of the planets of our solar system, I could tell you; but not knowing where Poloda is, I can only say that I do not know."

"Why did you appear naked in the limits of Orvis?" demanded one of the judges. Orvis is the name of the city into which I had been ruthlessly catapulted without clothes. "Is it possible that the inhabitants of this place you call America do not wear clothing?"

"They wear clothing, Most Honorable Judge," I replied (Harkas Yen had coached me in the etiquette of the courtroom and the proper way to address the judges); "but it varies with the mood of the wearer, the temperature, styles, and personal idiosyncrasies. I have seen ancient males wandering around a place called Palm Springs with nothing but a pair of shorts to hide their hairy obesity; I have seen beautiful women clothed up to the curve of the breast in the evening, who had covered only about one per centum of their bodies at the beach in the afternoon; but, Most Honorable Judge, I have never seen any female costume more revealing than those worn by the beautiful girls of Orvis. To answer your first question: I appeared in Orvis naked, because I had no clothes when I arrived here."

"You are excused for a moment," said the judge who had questioned me; then he turned to the seven old men, and asked them to take the stand. After they had been sworn and he had asked their names, the chief judge asked them if they could locate any such world as the Earth.

"We have questioned Harkas Yen, who has questioned the defendant," replied the oldest of the seven, "and we have come to this conclusion." After which followed half an hour of astronomical data. "This person," he finished, "came from a solar system that is beyond the range of our most powerful telescopes, and is probably about 22,000 light-years beyond Canapa."

That was staggering; but what was more staggering was when Harkas Yen convinced me that Canapa was identical with the globular cluster N. G. C. 7006, which is 220,000 light-years distant from the Earth and not just a measly 22,000; and then, to cap the climax, he explained that Poloda is 230,000 light-years from Canapa, which would locate me something like 450,000 light-years from Earth. As light travels 186,000 miles per second, I will let you figure how far Poloda is from Earth; but I may say that if a telescope on Poloda were powerful enough to see what was transpiring on Earth, it would see what was transpiring there 450,000 years ago.

After they had quizzed the seven astronomers, and

learned nothing, one of the judges called Balzo Maro to the stand; and the girl I had seen that first day in the garden arose from her seat and came forward to the witness stand.

After they had gone through the preliminaries, they questioned her about me. "He wore no clothes?" asked one of the judges.

"None," said Balzo Maro.

"Did he attempt to—ah—annoy you in any way?"

"No," said Balzo Maro.

"You know, don't you," asked one of the judges, "that for willfully annoying a woman, an alien can be sentenced to destruction?"

"Yes," said Balzo Maro; "but he did not annoy me. I watched him because I thought he might be a dangerous character, perhaps a Kapar spy; but I am convinced that he is what he claims to be."

I could have hugged Balzo Maro.

Now the judges said to me: "If you are convicted, you may be destroyed or imprisoned for the duration; but as the war has now gone into its one hundred and first year, such a sentence would be equivalent to death. We wish to be fair, and really there is nothing more against you than that you are an alien who spoke no tongue known upon Poloda."

"Then release me and let me serve Unis against her enemies."

CHAPTER THREE

THE JUDGES DISCUSSED my proposition in whispers for about ten minutes; then they put me on probation until the Janhai could decide the matter, and after that they turned me back to the custody of Harkas Yen, who told me later that a great honor had been done, as the Janhai rules Unis; it was like putting my case in the hands of the President of the United States or the King of England.

The Janhai is a commission composed of seven men who are elected to serve until they are seventy years old, when they may be reelected; the word is a compound of *jan* (seven) and *hai* (elect). Elections are held only when it is necessary to fill a vacancy on the Janhai, which appoints all judges and what corresponds to our governors of States, who, in turn, appoint all other State or provincial officials and the mayors of cities, the mayors appointing municipal officers. There are no ward heelers in Unis; no Tammany Hall; no Ohio Gang; no Kelly-Nash gang; no Hague of New Jersey.

Each member of the Janhai heads a department, of which there are seven: War; Foreign, which includes State; Commerce; Interior; Education; Treasury; and Justice. These seven men elect one of their own number every six years as Eljanhai, or High Commissioner. He is, in effect, the ruler of Unis; but he cannot serve two consecutive terms. These men, like all the appointees of the Janhai, the provincial governors, and the mayors, must submit to a very thorough intelligence test, which determines the candidate's native intelligence as well as his fund of acquired knowledge; and more weight is given the former than the latter.

I could not but compare this system with our own, under which it is not necessary for a Presidential candidate to be able either to read or write; even a congenital idiot could run for the Presidency of the United States of America, and serve if he were elected.

There were two cases following mine, and Harkas Yen wanted to stay and hear them. The first was a murder case; and the defendant had chosen to be tried before one judge, rather than a jury of five men.

"He is either innocent, or the killing was justifiable," remarked Harkas Yen; "when they are guilty, they usually ask for a jury trial."

In a fit of passion, the man had killed another who had broken up his home. In fifteen minutes, he was tried and acquitted.

The next case was that of the mayor of a small city who was accused of accepting a bribe. That case lasted about two hours and was tried before a jury of five men. In America, it would possibly have lasted two months. The judge made the attorneys stick to facts and the evidence. The jury was out not more than fifteen minutes, when it brought in a verdict of guilty. The judge sentenced the man to be shot on the morning of the fifth day. This gave him time to appeal the case to a court of five judges; they work fast in Unis.

Harkas Yen told me that the court of appeal would examine the transcript of the evidence and would probably confirm the finding of the lower court, unless the attorney for the defendant made an affidavit that he could bring in new evidence to clear his client. If he made such an affidavit, and the new evidence failed to alter the verdict, the attorney would forfeit his fee to the State and be compelled to pay all court costs for the second trial.

Attorneys' fees, like doctors', are fixed by law in Unis; and they are fair—a rich man pays a little more than a poor man, but they can't take his shirt. If a defendant is very poor, the State employs and pays any attorney the defendant may select; and the same plan is in effect for the services of doctors, surgeons, and hospitalization.

After the second trial, I went home with Harkas Yen and his son and daughter. While we were walking to the elevators, we heard the wail of sirens, and felt the building dropping down its shaft. It was precisely the same sensation I had when coming down in an elevator from the 102nd story of the Empire State Building.

This Justice Building, in which the trials had been held, is twenty stories high; and it dropped down to the bottom of its shaft in about twenty seconds. Pretty soon we heard the booming of antiaircraft guns and the terrific detonation of bombs.

"How long has this been going on?" I asked.

"All my life, and long before," replied Harkas Yen.

"This war is now in its one hundred and first year," said Harkas Don, his son. "We don't know anything else," he added, with a grin.

"It started about the time your grandfather was born," said Harkas Yen. "As a boy and young man, your great-grandfather lived in a happier world. Then, men lived and worked upon the surface of the planet; cities were built aboveground; but within ten years after the Kapars launched their campaign to conquer and rule the world, every city in Unis and every city in Kapar and many cities on others of the five continents were reduced to rubble.

"It was then that we started building these underground cities that can be raised or lowered by the power we derive from Omos." (The sun of Poloda.) "The Kapars have subjugated practically all the rest of Poloda; but we were, and still are, the richest nation in the world. What they have done to us, we have done to them; but they are much worse off than we. Their people live in underground warrens protected by steel and concrete; they subsist upon the foods raised by subjugated peoples who are no better than slaves, and work no better for hated masters; or they eat synthetic foods, as they wear synthetic clothing. They themselves produce nothing but the matériel of war. So heavily do we bomb and strafe their land that nothing can live upon its surface; but they keep on, for they know nothing but war. Periodically we offer them an honorable peace, but they will have nothing but the total destruction of Unis."

CHAPTER FOUR

HARKAS YEN INVITED me to remain in his home until some disposition of my case was made. His place is reached by an underground motorway a hundred feet beneath the surface. Throughout the city many buildings were still lowered, those more than a hundred feet high having entrances at this hundred-foot level as well as at ground level when they were raised. The smaller buildings were raised and lowered in shafts like our elevator shafts. Above them are thick slabs of armor plate which support the earth and topsoil in which grow the trees, shrubbery, and grass which hide them when they are lowered. When these smaller buildings are raised they come in contact with their protecting slabs and carry them on up with them.

After we left the center of the city I noticed many buildings built permanently at the hundred-foot level; and when I asked Harkas Yen about this, he explained that when this underground city had first been planned it was with the expectation that the war would soon be over and that the city could return to normal life at the surface; that when all hope of the war's end was abandoned, permanent underground construction was commenced.

"You can imagine," he continued, "the staggering expense involved in building these underground cities. The Janhai of Unis ordered them commenced eighty years ago and they are nowhere near completed yet. Hundreds of thousands of the citizens of Unis live in inadequate shelters, or just in caves or in holes dug in the ground. It is because of this terrific expense that, among other things, we wear these clothes we do. They are made of an indestructible plastic which resembles metal. No person, not even a member of the Janhai, may possess more than three suits, two for ordinary wear and one suit of working clothes, for all productivity must go into the construction of our cities and the prosecution of the war. Our efforts cannot be wasted in making clothes to meet every change in style and every silly vanity, as was true a hundred years ago. About the only things we have conserved from the old days, which are not absolutely essential to the winning of the war or the construction of our cities, are cultural. We would not permit art, music, and literature to die."

"It must be a hard life," I suggested, "especially for the women. Do you have no entertainment nor recreation at all?"

"Oh, yes," he replied, "but they are simple, and we do not devote much time to them. Our forebears who lived a hundred years ago would think it a very dull life, for they devoted most of their time to the pursuit of pleasure, which was one of the reasons that the Kapars prosecuted the war so successfully at first, and why almost every nation on Poloda, with the exception of Unis, was either subjugated or exterminated by the Kapars."

The motorcars of Unis are all identical, each one seating four people comfortably, or six uncomfortably. This standardization has effected a tremendous saving in labor and materials. Power is conducted to their motors by what we would call "radio" from central stations where the sun's energy is stored. As this source of power is inexhaustible, it has not been necessary to curtail the use of motors because of war needs. This same power is also used for operating the enormous pumps which are necessary for draining this underground world, the mechanism for raising the buildings, and the numerous air-conditioning plants which are necessary.

I was simply appalled by contemplation of the cost of the excavating and constructing of a world beneath the surface of the ground, and when I mentioned this to Harkas Yen he said: "There never has been enough wealth in the world to accomplish what we have accomplished, other than the potential wealth which is inherent in the people themselves. By the brains of our scientists and our leaders, by the unity of our people, and by the sweat of our brows we have done what we have done."

Harkas Yen's son and daughter, Don and Yamoda, accompanied us from the Hall of Justice to their home. Yamoda wore the gold sequins and red boots that all unmarried women wear, while Don was in the blue of the fighting forces. He and I have hit it off well together, both being fliers; and neither of us ever tire of hearing stories of the other's world. He has promised to try to get me into the flying service; and Harkas Yen thinks that it may be possible, as there is a constant demand for fliers to replace casualties, of which there are sometimes as many as five hundred thousand in a month.

These figures staggered me when Harkas Don first mentioned them, and I asked him how it was the nation had not long since been exterminated.

"Well, you see," he said, "they don't average as high as that. I think the statistics show that we lose on an average of about a hundred thousand men a month. There are sixteen million adult women in Unis and something like ten million babies are born every year. Probably a little better than half of these are boys. At least five million of them grow to maturity, for we are a very healthy race. So, you see, we can afford to lose a million men a year."

"I shouldn't think the mothers would like that very well," I said.

"Nobody does," he replied; "but it is war, and war is our way of life."

"In my country," I said, "we have what are known as

pacifists, and they have a song which is called, 'I didn't raise my boy to be a soldier.'"

Harkas Don laughed and then said what might be translated into English as: "If our women had a song, it would be, 'I didn't raise my son to be a slacker.'"

Harkas Yen's wife greeted me most cordially when I returned. She has been very lovely to me and calls me her other boy. She is a sad-faced woman of about sixty, who was married at seventeen and has had twenty children, six girls and fourteen boys. Thirteen of the boys have been killed in the war. Most of the older women of Unis, and the older men, too, have sad faces; but they never complain nor do they ever weep. Harkas Yen's wife told me that their tears were exhausted two generations ago.

CHAPTER FIVE

I DIDN'T GET INTO the flying service, I got into the Labor Corps; and, believe me, it was labor spelled with all caps, not just a capital L. I had wondered how they repaired the damage done by the continual bombing of the Kapars and I found out the first day I was inducted into the Corps. Immediately following the departure of the Kapar bombers we scurried out of holes in the ground like worker ants. There were literally thousands of us, and we were accompanied by trucks, motorized shovels, and scrapers, and an ingenious tool for lifting a tree out of the ground with the earth all nicely balled around the roots.

First, we filled the bomb craters, gathering up such plants and trees as might be saved. The trucks brought sod, trees, and plants that had been raised underground; and within a few hours all signs of the raid had been obliterated.

It seemed to me like a waste of energy; but one of my fellow workers explained to me that it had two important purposes—one was to maintain the morale of the Unisans, and the other was to lower the morale of the enemy.

We worked nine days and had one day off, the first day of their ten-day week. When we were not working on the surface we were working belowground; and as I was an unskilled laborer, I did enough work in my first month in the Labor Corps to last an ordinary man a lifetime. On my third day of rest, which came at the end of my first month in the Labor Corps, Harkas Don, who was also off duty on that day, suggested that we go to the mountains. He and Yamoda formed a little party of twelve. Three of the men were from the Labor Corps and the other three were in the fighting service. One of the girls was the daughter of the Eljanhai, whose office is practically that of the President. Two of the others were daughters of members of the Labor Corps. There was the daughter of a university president, the daughter of an army officer, and Yamoda. The sorrow and suffering of perpetual war has developed a national unity which has wiped out all class distinction.

Orvis stands on a plateau entirely surrounded by mountains, the nearest of which are about a hundred miles from the city; and it was to these mountains that we took an underground train. Here rise the highest peaks in the range that surrounds Orvis; and as the mountains at the east end of the plateau are low and a wide pass breaks the range at the west end, the Kapars usually come and go either from the east or west; so it is considered reasonably safe to take an outing on the surface at this location. I tell you it was good to get out in the sun again without having to work like a donkey. The country there was beautiful; there were mountain streams and there was a little lake beside which we planned to picnic in a grove of trees. They had selected the grove because the trees would hide us from any chance enemy fliers who might pass overhead. For all of the lives of four generations they have had to think of this until it is second nature for them to seek shelter when in the open.

Someone suggested that we swim before we eat. "I'd like nothing better," I said, "but I didn't bring any swimming things."

"What do you mean?" asked Yamoda.

"Why, I mean clothes to swim in—a swimming suit," I replied.

That made them all laugh. "You have your swimming suit on," said Harkas Don; "you were born in it."

I had lost most of my tan after living underground for a couple of months; but I was still very dark compared with these white-skinned people who have lived like moles for almost four generations, and my head of black hair contrasted strangely with the copper hair of the girls and the blond hair of the men.

The water was cold and refreshing and we came out with enormous appetites. After we had eaten we lay around on the grass; and they sang the songs that they liked.

Time passed rapidly and we were all startled when one of the men stood up and announced that we had better leave for home. He had scarcely finished speaking when we heard the report of a pistol shot and saw him pitch forward upon his face, dead.

The three soldiers with us were the only ones who bore arms. They ordered us to lie flat on our faces, and then they crept forward in the direction from which the sound of the pistol shot had come. They disappeared in the underbrush and shortly afterward we heard a fusillade of shots. This was more than I could stand, lying there like a scared rabbit while Harkas Don and his companions were out there fighting; so I crawled after them.

I came up to them on the edge of a little depression in which were perhaps a dozen men behind an outcropping of rock which gave them excellent protection. Harkas Don and his companions were concealed from the enemy by shrubbery, but not protected by it. Every time an enemy showed any part of his body one of the three would fire. Finally the man behind the extreme right end of the barrier exposed himself for too long, and we were so close that I could see the hole the bullet made in his forehead before he fell back behind the barrier. Beyond the point where he fell thick trees and underbrush concealed the continuation of the outcropping, if there was more, and this gave me an idea which I immediately set to work to put into execution.

I slipped backward a few yards into the underbrush and then crawled cautiously to the right. Taking advantage of this excellent cover, I circled around until I was opposite the left flank of the enemy; then I wormed myself forward on my belly inch by inch until through a tiny opening in the underbrush I saw the body of the dead man and, beyond it, his companions behind their rocky barrier. They were all dressed in drab, gray uniforms that looked like coveralls, and they wore gray metal helmets that covered their entire heads and the backs of their necks, leaving only their faces exposed. They had crossed shoulder belts and a waist belt filled with cartridges in clips of about fifteen. Their complexions were sallow and unwholesome; and though I knew that they must be young men, they looked old; and the faces of all of them seemed set in sullen scowls. They were the first Kapars that I had seen, but I recognized them instantly from descriptions that Harkas Don and others had given me.

The pistol of the dead man (it was really a small machine gun) lay at his side, and there was almost a full clip of cartridges in it. I could see them plainly from where I lay. I pushed forward another inch or two and then one of the Kapars turned and looked in my direction. At first I thought that he had discovered me, but I presently saw that he was looking at his dead comrade. Then he turned and spoke to his companions in a language I could not understand; it sounded to me something like the noise that pigs make when they eat. One of them nodded to him, evidently in assent, and he turned and started to walk toward the dead man.

That looked like the end of my little scheme, and I was just about to take a desperate chance and make a lunge for the pistol when the Kapar foolishly permitted his head to show above the top of the barrier, and down he went with a bullet in his head. The other Kapars looked at him and jabbered angrily to one another; and while they were jabbering I took the chance, extended my arm through the underbrush, grasped the pistol and dragged it slowly toward me.

The Kapars were still arguing, or scolding, or whatever they were doing, when I took careful aim at the nearest of them and commenced firing. Four of the ten went down before the others realized from what direction the attack was coming. Two of them started firing at the underbrush where I was hidden; but I brought them down, and then the other four broke and ran. In doing so they were exposed to the fire of Harkas Don and his companions, as well as of mine, and we got every one of them.

I had crawled out from the underbrush in order to take better aim, and now I did not dare stand up for fear my friends would get me before they recognized me; so I called Harkas Don by name and presently he answered.

"Who are you?" he demanded.

"Tangor," I replied. "I'm coming out; don't shoot."

They came over to me then, and we went in search of the Kapar ship, which we knew must be nearby. We found it in a little natural clearing, half a mile back from the place where we had shot them. It was unguarded; so we were sure that we had got them all.

"We are ahead twelve pistols, a lot of ammunition, and one ship," I said.

"We will take the pistols and ammunition back," said Harkas Don, "but no one can fly this ship back to Orvis without being killed."

He found a heavy tool in the ship and demolished the motor.

Our little outing was over; and we went home, carrying our one dead with us.

CHAPTER SIX

THE NEXT DAY, while I was loading garbage on a train that was going to the incinerator, a boy in yellow sequins came and spoke to the man in charge of us, who turned and called to me. "You are ordered to report to the office of the Commissioner for War," he said; "this messenger will take you."

"Hadn't I better change my clothes?" I asked. "I imagine that I don't smell very good."

The boss laughed. "The Commissioner for War has smelled garbage before," he said, "and he doesn't like to be kept waiting." So I went along with the yellow-clad messenger to the big building called the House of the Janhai, which houses the government of Unis.

I was conducted to the office of one of the Commissioner's assistants.

He looked up as we entered. "What do you want?" he demanded.

"This is the man for whom you sent me," replied the messenger.

"Oh, yes, your name is Tangor. I might have known by that black hair. So you're the man who says that he comes from another world, some 548,000 light-years from Poloda."

I said that I was. Poloda is 450,000 light-years from Earth by our reckoning, but it is 547,500 Polodian light-years, as there are only three hundred days in a

Polodian year; but what's one hundred thousand light-years among friends, anyway?

"Your exploit of yesterday with the Kapars has been reported to me," said the officer, "as was also the fact that you were a flier in your own world, and that you wish to fly for Unis."

"That is right, sir," I said.

"In view of the cleverness and courage which you displayed yesterday, I am going to permit you to train for the flying force—if you think you would prefer that to shoveling garbage," he added with a smile.

"I have no complaint to make about shoveling garbage, or anything else that I am required to do in Unis, sir," I replied. "I came here an uninvited guest, and I have been treated extremely well. I would not complain of any service that might be required of me."

"I am glad to hear you say that," he said. Then he handed me an order for a uniform, and gave me directions as to where and to whom to report after I had obtained it.

The officer to whom I reported sent me first to a factory manufacturing pursuit-plane motors, where I remained a week; that is, nine working days. There are ten assembly lines in this plant and a completed motor comes off of each of them every hour for ten hours a day. As there are twenty-seven working days in the Polodian month, this plant was turning out twenty-seven hundred motors a month. From this factory I was sent to a fuselage and assembly plant, which was operated on precisely the same time schedule, with an output of twenty-seven hundred completed planes a month.

The science of aerodynamics, whether on Earth or on Poloda, is governed by certain fixed natural laws; so that Polodian aircraft do not differ materially in appearance from those with which I was familiar on Earth, but their construction is radically different from ours because of their development of a light, practically indestructible, rigid plastic of enormous strength. Huge machines stamp out fuselage and wings from this plastic. The parts are then rigidly joined together and the seams hermetically sealed. The fuselage has a double wall with an air space between, and the wings are hollow.

On completion of the plane the air is withdrawn from the space between the walls of the fuselage and from the interior of the wings, the resulting vacuum giving the ship considerable lifting power, which greatly increases the load that it can carry. They are not lighter than air, but when not heavily loaded they can be maneuvered and landed very slowly.

There are forty of these plants, ten devoted to the manufacture of heavy bombers, ten to light bombers, ten to combat planes, and ten to pursuit planes, which are also used for reconnaissance. The enormous output of these factories, over a hundred thousand planes a month, is necessary to replace lost and worn-out planes, as well as to increase the fighting force, which is the aim of the Unisan government.

As I had in the engine factory, I remained in this factory nine days as an observer, and then I was sent back to the engine factory and put to work for two weeks; then followed two weeks in the fuselage and assembly plants, after which I had three weeks of flying instruction, which on several occasions was interrupted by Kapar raids, resulting in dogfights in which my instructor and I took part.

During this period of instruction I was studying the four of the five principal languages of Poloda with which I was not familiar, giving special attention to the language of the Kapars. I also spent much time studying the geography of Poloda.

All during this period I had no recreation whatsoever, often studying all night until far into the morning; so when I was finally awarded the insignia of a flier, I was glad to have a day off. As I was now living in barracks, I had seen nothing of the Harkases; and so, on this, my first free day, I made a beeline for their house.

Balzo Maro, the girl who had been first to discover me on my arrival on Poloda, was there, with Yamoda and Don. They all seemed genuinely glad to see me and congratulated me on my induction into the flying service.

"You look very different from the first time I saw you," said Balzo Maro, with a smile; and I certainly did, for I was wearing the blue sequins, the blue boots, and the blue helmet of the fighting service.

"I have learned a number of things since I came to Poloda," I told her, "and after having enjoyed a swimming party with a number of young men and women, I cannot understand why you were so shocked at my appearance that day."

Balzo Maro laughed. "There is quite a difference between swimming and running around the city of Orvis that way," she said, "but really it was not that which shocked me. It was your brown skin and your black hair. I didn't know what sort of wild creature you might be."

"Well, you know when I saw you running around in that fancy dress costume in the middle of the day, I thought there might be something wrong with you."

"There is nothing fancy about this," she said. "All the girls wear the same thing. Don't you like it—don't you think it's pretty?"

"Very," I said; "but don't you tire of always wearing the same thing? Don't you sometimes long for a new costume?"

Balzo Maro shook her head. "It is war," she said; the universal answer to almost everything on Poloda.

"We may do our hair as we please," said Harkas Yamoda, "and that is something."

"I suppose you have hairdressers who are constantly inventing new styles," I said.

Yamoda laughed. "Nearly a hundred years ago," she said, "the hairdressers, the cosmeticians, and the beauticians

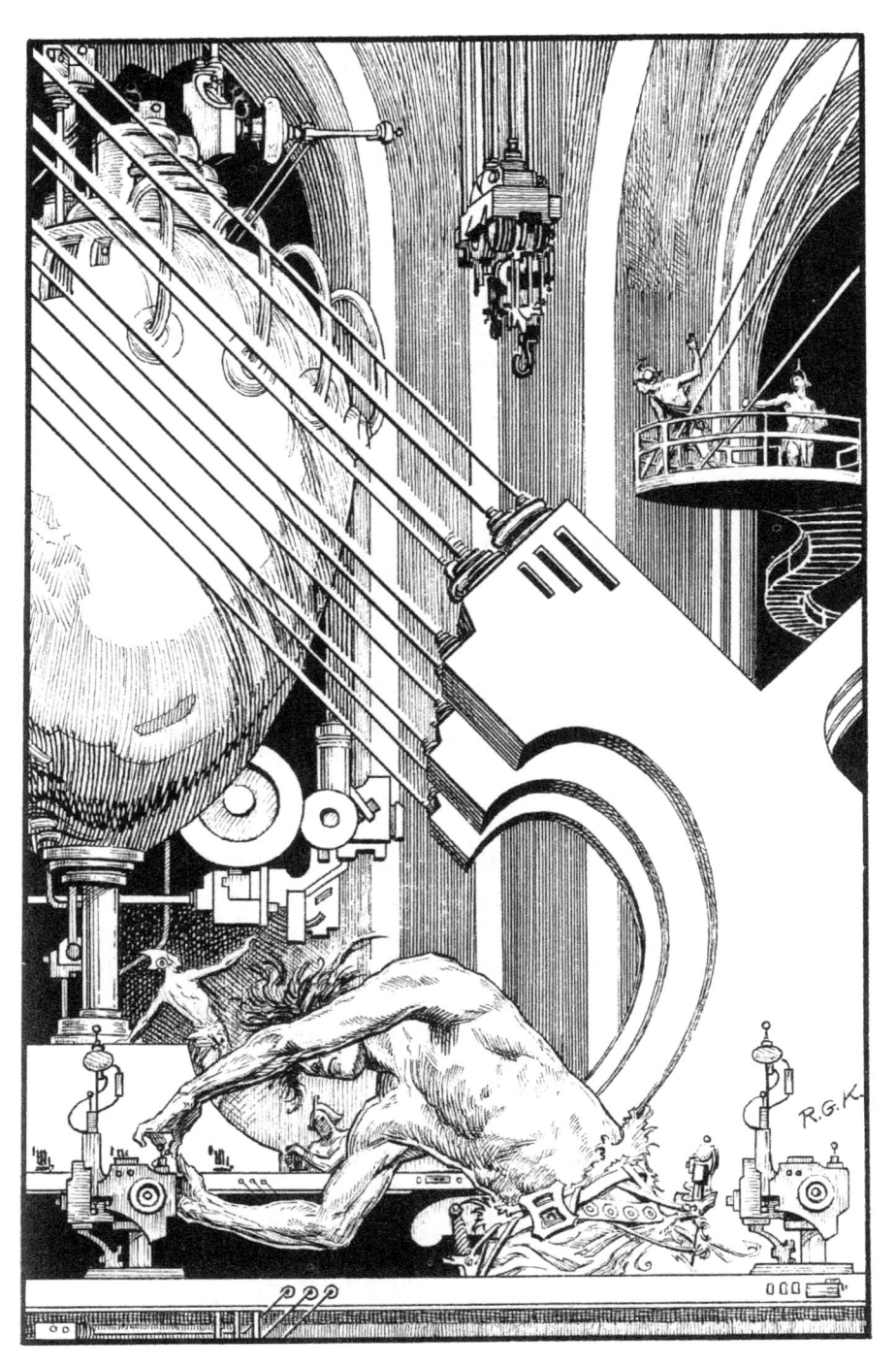

"I was sent back to the engine factory."

went into the fields to work for Unis. What we do, we do ourselves."

"You all work, don't you?" I asked.

"Yes," said Balzo Maro; "we work that we may release men for men's work in the fighting service and the Labor Corps."

I could not but wonder what American women would do if the Nazis succeeded in bringing total war to their world. I think that they would arise to the emergency just as courageously as have the women of Unis, but it might be a little galling to them at first to wear the same indestructible costume from the time they got their growth until they were married; a costume that, like Balzo Maro's, as she told me, might be as much as fifty years old, and which had been sold and resold time and time again as each wearer had no further use for it. And then, when they were married, to wear a similar, indestructible silver costume for the rest of their lives, or until their husbands were killed in battle, when they would change to purple. Doubtless, Irene, Hattie Carnegie, Valentina, and Adrian, would all commit suicide, along with Max Factor, Perc Westmore, and Elizabeth Arden. It was rather a strain on my imagination to visualize Elizabeth Arden hoeing potatoes.

"You have been here several months now," said Harkas Don; "how do you like our world by this time?"

"I don't have to tell you that I like the people who live in it," I replied. "Your courage and morale are magnificent. I like your form of government, too. It is simple and efficient, and seems to have developed a unified people without criminals or traitors."

Harkas Don shook his head. "You are wrong there," he said; "we have criminals and we have traitors, but unquestionably far fewer than in the world of a hundred years ago, when there was a great deal of political corruption, which always goes hand in hand with crimes of other kinds. There are many Kapar sympathizers among us, and some full-blooded Kapars who have been sent here to direct espionage and sabotage. They are constantly dropping down by night with parachutes. We get most of them, but not all. You see, they are a mixed race and there are many with white skins and blond hair who might easily pass for Unisans."

"And there are some with black hair, too," said Harkas Yamoda, as she looked at me meaningly, but softened it with a smile.

"It's strange I was not taken for a Kapar, then, and destroyed," I said.

"It was your dark skin that saved you," said Harkas Don, "and the fact that you unquestionably understood no language on Poloda. You see, they made some tests, of which you were not aware because you did not understand any of the languages. Had you, you could not have helped but show some reaction."

Later, while we were eating the noonday meal, I remarked that for complete war between nations possessing possibly millions of fighting ships, the attacks of the Kapars since I had been in Unis had not seemed very severe.

"We have lulls like this occasionally," said Harkas Don. "It is as though both sides became simultaneously tired of war, but one never can tell when it will break out again in all its fury."

He scarcely had ceased speaking when there came a single, high-pitched shrieking note from the loudspeakers that are installed the length and breadth of the underground city. Harkas Don rose. "There it is now," he said. "The general alarm. You will see war now, Tangor, my friend. Come."

We hurried to the car, and the girls came with us to bring the car back after they had delivered us to our stations.

Hundreds of ramps lead to the surface from the underground airdromes of Orvis, and from their camouflaged openings at the surface planes zoom out and up at the rate of twenty a minute, one every three seconds, like winged termites emerging from a wooden beam.

I was flying a ship in a squadron of pursuit planes. It was armed with four guns. One I fired through the propeller shaft, there were two in an after cockpit, which could be swung in any direction, and a fourth which fired down through the bottom of the fuselage.

As I zoomed out into the open the sky was already black with our ships. The squadrons were forming quickly and streaking away toward the southwest, to meet the Kapars who would be coming in from that direction. And presently I saw them, like a black mass of gnats miles away.

CHAPTER SEVEN

OF COURSE, at the time that I had been killed in our little war down on Earth, there had not been a great deal of aerial activity; I mean, no great mass flights. I know there was talk that either side might send over hundreds of ships in a single flight, and hundreds of ships seemed a lot of ships; but this day, as I followed my squadron commander into battle, there were more than ten thousand ships visible in the sky; and this was only the first wave. We were climbing steadily at terrific speed in an effort to get above the Kapars, and they were doing the same. We made contact about twelve miles above the ground, and the battle soon after developed into a multitude of individual dogfights, notwithstanding the fact that both sides tried to keep some semblance of formation.

The atmosphere of Poloda rises about one hundred miles above the planet, and one can fly up to an altitude of about fifteen miles without needing an oxygen tank.

In a few minutes I became separated from my squadron and found myself engaged with three light Kapar combat planes. Ships were falling all around us, like dead leaves in an autumn storm; and so crowded was the sky with fighting ships that much of my attention had to be concentrated upon avoiding collisions; but I succeeded in maneuvering into a commanding position and had the satisfaction of seeing one of the Kapars roll over and plummet toward the ground. The other two were now at a disadvantage, as I was still above them; and they turned tail and started for home. My ship was very much faster than one of theirs, and I soon overhauled the laggard and shot him down, too.

I could not but recall my last engagement, when I shot down two of three Messerschmitts before being shot down myself; and I wondered if this were to be a repetition of that adventure—was I to die a second time?

I chased the remaining Kapar out over the enormous bay that indents the west coast of Unis. It is called the Bay of Hagar. It is really a gulf, for it is fully twelve hundred miles long. An enormous island at its mouth has been built up with the earth excavated from the underground workings of Unis, pumped there through a pipe that you could drive an automobile through.

It was between the coast and this island that I got on the tail of this last Kapar. One gunner was hanging dead over the edge of the cockpit, but the other was working his gun. Above the barking of my own gun I could hear his bullets screaming past me; and why I wasn't hit I shall never know, unless it was that that Kapar was Poloda's worst marksman.

Evidently I wasn't much better, but finally I saw him slump down into the cockpit; and then beyond his ship I saw another wave of Kapar fliers coming, and I felt that it was a good time to get away from there. The Kapar pilot that I had been pursuing must have seen the new wave at the same time that I did, for he turned immediately after I had turned and pursued me. And now my engine began to give trouble; it must have been hit by the last spurt from the dead gunner's piece. The Kapar was overhauling me, and he was getting in range, but there was no answering fire from the gunners in my after cockpit. I glanced back to find that they were both dead.

Now I was in a fix, absolutely defenseless against the ship pulling up behind me. I figured I might pull a fast one on him; so I banked steeply and dove beneath him; then I banked again and came up under his tail with my gun bearing on his belly. I was firing bullets into him when he dived to escape me, but he never came out of that dive.

To the west the sky was black with Kapar ships. In a minute they would be upon me; it was at that moment that my engine gave up the ghost. Ten or eleven miles below me was the coast of Unis. A thousand miles to the northeast was Orvis. I might have glided 175 or 180 miles toward the city, but the Kapars would long since have been over me and some of their ships would have been detached to come down and put an end to me. As they might already have sighted me, I put the ship into a spin in the hope of misleading them into thinking I had been shot down. I spun down for a short distance and then went into a straight dive, and I can tell you that spinning and diving for ten or eleven miles is an experience.

I brought the ship down between the coast and a range of mountains, and no Kapar followed me. As I climbed out of the pilot's cockpit, Bantor Han, the third gunner, emerged from the ship.

"Nice work," he said, "we got all three of them."

"We had a bit of luck," I said, "and now we've got a long walk to Orvis."

"We'll never see Orvis again," said the gunner.

"What do you mean?" I demanded.

"This coast has been right in the path of Kapar flights for a hundred years. Where we are standing was once one of the largest cities of Unis, a great seaport. Can you find a stick or stone of it now? And for two or three hundred miles inland it is the same; nothing but bomb craters."

"But are there no cities in this part of Unis?" I asked.

"There are some farther south. The nearest is about a thousand miles from here, and on the other side of this range of mountains. There are cities far to the north, and cities east of Orvis; but it has never been practical to build even underground cities directly in the path of the Kapar flights, while there are other sections less affected."

"Well," I said, "I am not going to give up so easily. I will at least try to get to Orvis or some other city. Suppose we try for the one on the other side of these mountains. At least we won't be in the path of the Kapars every time they come over."

Bantor Han shook his head again. "Those mountains are full of wild beasts," he said. "There was a very large collection of wild animals in the city of Hagar when the war broke out over a hundred years ago. Many of them were killed in the first bombing of the city; but all their barriers were broken down, and the survivors escaped. For a hundred years they have ranged these mountains and they have multiplied. The inhabitants of Polan, this city you wish to try to reach, scarcely dare stick their heads aboveground because of them. No," he continued, "we have no complaint to make. You and I will die here, and that will mean that we have lost four men and one pursuit plane to their three light combat ships and, possibly, twenty men. It is a mighty good day's work, Tangor, and you should be proud."

"That is what I call patriotism and loyalty," I said; "but I can be just as patriotic and loyal alive as dead, and I don't intend even to think of giving up yet. If we are going to die anyway, I can see no advantage in sitting here and starving to death. It would be far more interesting to have a little excitement thrown in."

Bantor Han shrugged. "That suits me," he said. "I thought I was as good as dead when you tackled those three combat planes, and the chances are that I should have been killed in my next engagement. I have been too lucky; so, if you prefer to go and look for death instead of waiting for it to come to you, I'll trot along with you."

So Bantor Han and I took the weapons and ammunition of our dead comrades and entered the Mountains of Loras.

CHAPTER EIGHT

I WAS AMAZED by the beauty of these mountains after we entered them. We were about eight or nine hundred miles north of the equator and the climate was similar to the south temperate zone of Earth in summertime. Everything was green and beautiful, with a profusion of the strange trees and plants and flowers which are so like those of Earth, and yet so unlike. I had been cooped up for so long in the underground city of Orvis that I felt like a boy just released from a schoolroom for a long vacation. But Bantor Han was uneasy. "Of course, I was born here in Unis," he said, "but being on the surface like this is to me like being in a strange world, for I have spent practically all of my life either underground or high up in the air."

"Don't you think that this is beautiful?" I asked him.

"Yes," he said, "I suppose it is, but it is a little bewildering; there is so much of it. There is a feeling of rest, and quiet, and security down there in underground Orvis; and I am always glad to get back to it after a flight."

I suppose that was the result of living underground for generations, and that Bantor Han had developed a complex the exact opposite of claustrophobia. Possibly it has a name, but if it has I never heard it. There were streams in the mountains, and little lakes where we saw fish playing, and the first animal that we saw appeared to be some sort of an antelope. It was armed with long, sharp horns, and looked something like an addax. It was standing with its forefeet in shallow water at the edge of a lake, drinking, when we came upon it; and as it was upwind from us it did not catch our scent. When I saw it I drew Bantor Han into the concealment of some bushes.

"There is food," I whispered, and Bantor Han nodded.

I took careful aim and brought the animal down with a single bullet through the heart. We were busy carving a few steaks from it when our attention was attracted by a most unpleasant growl. We looked up simultaneously.

"That's what I meant," said Bantor Han. "The mountains are full of creatures like that."

Like most of the animals that I have seen on Poloda, it did not differ greatly from those on Earth; that is, they all have four legs, and two eyes, and usually a tail. Some are covered with hair, some with wool, some with fur, and some are hairless. The Polodian horse has three-toed feet, and a little horn in the center of his forehead. The cattle have no horns, nor are their hooves cloven. In fighting they bite and kick like an earthly horse. They are not horses and cows at all, but I call them by earthly names because of the purposes for which they are used. The horses are the saddle animals and beasts of burden, and occasionally are used for food. The cattle are definitely beef animals, and the cows give milk.

The creature that was creeping toward us with menacing growls was built like a lion and striped like a zebra, and it was about the size of an African lion. I drew my pistol from its holster, but Bantor Han laid a hand upon my arm. "Don't shoot it," he said, "you may make it angry. If we go away and leave this meat to it, it probably will not attack us."

"If you think I am going to leave our supper to that thing, you are very much mistaken," I said. I was amazed at Bantor Han. I knew that he was no coward. He had an excellent record in the fighting service and was covered with decorations. I think he was simply bewildered. Everything here on the ground was so new and strange to him. Put him twelve miles up in the air, or a hundred feet underground, and he wouldn't have backed down for man or beast.

I shook his hand off and took careful aim just as the creature charged, with a charge for all the world like an African lion. I let him have it straight in the heart—a stream of four or five bullets, and they almost tore him apart, for they were explosive bullets.

Civilized, cultured, as these Unisans are, they use both dumdum and exploding projectiles in their small arms. When I commented on the fact to one of them, he replied, "This is the complete war that the Kapars asked for."

"Well," exclaimed Bantor Han, "you did it, didn't you?" He seemed surprised that I had killed the beast.

We cooked and ate the antelope steaks, and left the rest where it lay, for we had no means of carrying any of it with us. We felt much refreshed, and I think that Bantor Han felt a little safer now that he had found that we were not going to be eaten up by the first carnivorous animal that we met.

It took us two days to cross through this mountain range. Fortunately for us, we had tackled it near its extreme northern end, where it was quite narrow and the mountains were little more than large hills. We had plenty to eat, and were only attacked twice more by dangerous animals, once by a huge creature that resembled a hyena, and again by the beast that I have named "the lion of Poloda." The two nights were the worst, because of the increased danger of prowling carnivora. The first we spent in a cave, and took turns standing watch, and the second night we slept in the open; but luck was with us and nothing attacked us.

As we came down out of a canyon on the east side of the mountains we saw that which brought us to a sudden stop—a Kapar plane not half a mile from us, on the edge of a little ravine that was a continuation of the canyon we were in. There were two men beside the plane, and they seemed to be digging in the ground.

"Two more Kapars for our bag, Bantor Han," I said. "Come on."

"If we get them and destroy their plane, we can certainly afford to die," he said.

"You're always wanting to die," I said reproachfully. "I intend to live." He would have been surprised had he known I was already dead, and buried somewhere 548,000 light-years away! "And furthermore, Bantor Han," I added, "we are not going to destroy that plane; not if it will fly."

We dropped into the ravine and made our way down toward the Kapars. We were entirely concealed from above, and if we made any noise it was drowned out by the noise of the little brook running over its rocky bed at the bottom of the ravine.

When I thought we had gone far enough, I told Bantor Han to wait and then I clambered up the side of the ravine to reconnoiter. Sure enough, I had hit the nail right on the head. There were the two Kapars digging away, scarcely a hundred feet from me. I crouched down and beckoned Bantor Han to come up.

There is no chivalry in complete war, I can assure you. Those two Kapars didn't have a chance. They were both dead before they knew there was an enemy within a thousand miles. Then we went to see what they had been at, and found a box beside the hole which they had been excavating. It was a metal box with a waterproof top, and when we opened it we found that it contained two complete blue uniforms of the Unis Fighting Corps, together with helmets, boots, ammunition belts, daggers, and guns. There were also directions in the Kapar language for entering the city of Orvis and starting numerous fires on a certain night about a month later. Even the location of the buildings that might most easily be fired, and from which the fires would spread most rapidly, was given.

"I let him have it straight in the heart."

We put the box aboard the ship and climbed in.

"We'll never make it," said Bantor Han. "We're bound to be shot down."

"You're certainly determined to die, aren't you?" I said, as I started the engine and taxied for the takeoff.

CHAPTER NINE

I KNEW THAT the sound detectors were already giving warning of the approach of a ship, and of a Kapar ship, too; for our ships are equipped with a secret device which permits the detectors to recognize them. The signal that it gives can be changed at will, and is changed every day, so that it really amounts to a countersign. Watchers must be on the alert for even a single ship, but I was positive that they would be looking up in the air, and so I hugged the ground, flying at an elevation of little more than twenty feet.

Before we reached the mountains which surround Orvis, I saw a squadron of pursuit planes come over the summit.

"They are looking for us," I said to Bantor Han, who was in the after cockpit, "and I'm going right up where they can see us."

"You'll come down in a hurry," said Bantor Han. I have never known such a pessimist.

"Now, listen," I said; "as soon as we get where you can distinguish the gunners and pilots and see that their uniforms are blue, you stand up and wave something, for if you can see the color of their uniforms, they can see the color of yours; and I don't believe they will shoot us down then."

"That's where you're mistaken," said Bantor Han; "lots of Kapars have tried to enter Orvis in uniforms taken from our dead pilots."

"Don't forget to stand up and wave," I said.

We were getting close now, and it was a tense moment. I could plainly see the blue uniforms of the gunners and the pilots; and they could certainly see Bantor Han's and mine, and with Bantor Han waving to them they must realize that here was something unusual.

Presently the Squadron Commander ordered his ships to take position above us; and then he commenced to circle us, coming closer and closer. He came so close at last that our wings almost touched.

"Who are you?" he demanded.

"Bantor Han and Tangor," I replied, "in a captured Kapar ship."

I heard one of his gunners say, "Yes, that's Bantor Han. I know him well."

"Land just south of the city," said the Squadron Commander. "We'll escort you down; otherwise you'll be shot down."

I signaled that I understood, and he said, "Follow me." So we dropped down toward Orvis near the apex of a V-formation, and I can tell you I was mighty glad to pile out of that ship with a whole skin.

"I'm afraid you are going to die a natural death, Bantor Han," I said to my companion.

"Oh, no," he said, "I may be killed on my next flight." He was hopeless.

I told the Squadron Commander about what we had seen the two Kapars doing, and turned the box over to him. Then I went and reported to my own squadron commander.

"I never expected to see you again," he said. "What luck did you have?"

"Twenty-two Kapars and four ships," I replied.

He looked at me a bit skeptically. "All by yourself?"

"There were three in my crew," I said. "I lost two of them, and my ship."

"The balance is still very much in your favor," he said. "Who else survived?"

"Bantor Han," I replied.

"A good man," he said; "where is he?"

"Waiting outside, sir."

He summoned Bantor Han. "I understand you had very good luck," he said.

"Yes sir," said Bantor Han; "four ships and twenty-two men, though we lost two men and our ship."

"I shall recommend decorations for both of you," he said, and dismissed us. I asked to leave to go to the home of Harkas Yen, and it was granted.

"You may take a day off," he said, "you have earned it; and you, too, Bantor Han."

I lost no time in setting off to the Harkases. Harkas Yamoda was in the garden. She was just sitting there staring at the ground and looking very sad; but when I spoke her name she leaped to her feet and came running toward me, laughing almost hysterically. She seized me by both arms and shook me.

"Oh, Tangor," she cried, "you did not come back, and we were sure that you had been shot down. The last that anyone saw of you, you were fighting three Kapar combat planes alone."

"Harkas Don," I asked, "he came back?"

"Yes; now we shall all be so thankful and so happy—until next time."

I had dinner with Yamoda and her father and mother, and after dinner Harkas Don came. He was as surprised and delighted as the others to see me.

"I didn't think you had a chance," he said. "When a man is gone three days, he is reported dead. You were very fortunate."

He was a little envious of me when I told him of our big-game shooting in the Mountains of Loras. All his life he has heard of the wild animals there, but he never had the opportunity to visit the mountains, although he had flown over them often. The people of Unis don't take time off to go big-game hunting. Every tenth day they get a day off, and it is that way from the time they are fifteen years old until they are too old to work or fight. Then they go quietly out of the city, and are seen no more. They don't all do that, because it is not required, and the government takes good care of the oldsters who can no longer work and support themselves. But it is the choice of many, largely, I think, because they are tired of living in a world constantly at war. They pine for quiet, and rest, and peace; and from the moment that they are born the only place that they can hope to find it is in a grave.

"How did the battle go, Harkas Don?" I asked.

"We thrashed them as usual," he said. "We have better ships, better pilots, better gunners, better guns, and I think that now we have more ships. I don't know why they keep on coming over. They sent over two waves of five thousand ships each this time, and we shot down at least five thousand of them. We lost a thousand ships and two thousand men. The others parachuted to safety."

"I don't see why they keep it up," I said. "I shouldn't think they'd be able to get men to fight when they know they are just going to their death for no good reason."

"They are afraid of their masters," replied Harkas Don, "and they have been regimented for so many years that they have no initiative and no individuality. Another reason is that they wish to eat. The leaders live like princes of old; the army officers live exceptionally well; and the soldiers get plenty to eat, such as it is. If they were not fighting men, they would be laborers, which, in Kapara, is the equivalent of being a slave. They get barely enough food to subsist upon and they work from sixteen to eighteen hours a day; yet their lot is infinitely better than that of the subjugated peoples, many of whom have been reduced to cannibalism. Under military guards they are forced to work in the fields in their native lands, but what they produce is taken from them and sent to Kapara. It has been a common report for years that our dead who fall over there are shipped to these people for food. That," he concluded, "is complete war."

"Let's talk of something pleasant," said Yamoda.

"I think I see something pleasant to talk about coming," I said, nodding toward the entrance to the garden where we were sitting. It was Balzo Maro.

She came in with a brilliant smile, which I could see was forced. Harkas Don met her and took both her hands and pressed them, and Yamoda kissed her. I had never seen such demonstrations of affection before, for though those three people loved one another, and each knew it, they made no show of that love in front of others.

They evidently saw that I was puzzled, and Balzo Maro said, "My youngest brother died gloriously in the battle"; and after a pause she said, "It is war." I am not terribly emotional, but a lump came in my throat and tears to my eyes. These brave people! How they have suffered because of the greed for power, the vanity, and the hate of a man who died almost a hundred years ago!

They did not speak of Balzo Maro's loss again; they never would speak of it again; the dead are dead. Tomorrow another thousand or two thousand may die; but the living must go on living, and working, and fighting, and dying. It is war.

"So you have tomorrow free," said Harkas Don. "Perhaps you are fortunate."

"Why?" I asked.

"Tomorrow we raid Kapara with twenty thousand ships," he said. "It is a reprisal raid."

"And then they will send over forty thousand ships in reprisal," said Harkas Yamoda; "and so it goes on forever and ever."

"I shall not have a free day tomorrow," I said.

"Why, what do you mean?" asked Yamoda.

"I am going out with my squadron," I said. "I don't see why the commander didn't tell me."

"Because you have earned a day to yourself," said Harkas Don.

"Nevertheless, I am going," I said.

"You would be very foolish," he replied. "When you get a free day, take it. You will have plenty of opportunity to be killed the next day, or the day thereafter."

"Please don't go," said Harkas Yamoda.

I laughed. "Oh, don't worry about me," I said. "I'll come back." I wanted to tell them that I was already dead, and that people couldn't be killed twice, but as a matter of fact I wasn't so sure of it myself. I had long since pricked myself with a knife to see if I were really alive, and it had hurt, and blood had flowed; so I had to conclude that I might die again. It might be very awkward on the day of resurrection to have one of me bobbing up from the Rhine Valley and the other one from Poloda.

CHAPTER TEN

WE TOOK OFF the next morning just before dawn, ten thousand planes of all descriptions. We were to fly at an altitude of twelve miles, and as we gained it, four of Omos' eleven planets were visible in the heavens, the nearest less than six hundred thousand miles away. It was a gorgeous sight indeed. Around Omos, the sun of this system, revolve eleven planets, each approximately the size of our Earth. They are spaced almost exactly equidistant from one another; the path of their orbits being a million miles from the center of the sun, which is much smaller than the sun of our own solar system. An atmospheric belt seventy-two hundred miles in diameter revolves with the planets in the same orbit, thus connecting the planets by an air lane which offers the suggestion of possible interplanetary travel, which Harkas Yen told me would probably have been achieved long since had it not been for the war.

Ever since I came to Poloda my imagination has been intrigued by thoughts of the possibilities inherent in a visit to these other planets, where conditions almost identical with those on Poloda must exist. On these other planets there may be, and probably are, animal and plant life not dissimilar from our own, but which there is little likelihood that we shall ever see while complete war is maintained upon Poloda. The one great obstacle to interplanetary travel by Polodians is the fact that their motors are powered by wireless from central power stations, and it is estimated that at present the transmitting devices would not be efficient enough to power an engine much more than halfway to the nearest planet.

I had a long flight ahead of me, and speculating on interplanetary travel helped to pass the time away. Kapara lies on the continent of Epris, and Ergos, the capital of Kapara, is some eleven thousand miles from Orvis; and as our slowest planes have a speed of five hundred miles an hour, we were due over Ergos a couple of hours before dawn of the following day. As all three of my gunners are relief pilots, we relieved each other every four hours. Bantor Han was not with me on this flight, and I had three men with whom I had not previously flown. However, like all of the men of the fighting forces of Unis, they were efficient and dependable.

After crossing the coastline of Unis we flew 3,500 miles over the great Karagan Ocean, which extends for 8,500 miles from the northern continent of Karis to the southernmost tip of Unis, where the continents of Epris and Unis almost meet.

At an altitude of twelve miles there is not much to see but atmosphere. Occasional cloud banks floated beneath us, and between them we could see the blue ocean, scintillating in the sunlight, looking almost as smooth as a millpond; but the scintillation told us that high seas were running.

About noon we sighted the shore of Epris; and shortly after, a wave of Kapar planes came to meet us. There were not more than a thousand of them in this wave; and we drove them back, destroying about half of them, before a second and much larger wave attacked us. The fighting was furious, but most of our bombers got through. Our squadron was escorting one of the heavy bombers, and we were constantly engaged in fighting off enemy attack planes. My plane was engaged in three dogfights within half an hour, and I was fortunate to come through with the loss of only one man, one of the gunners in the after cockpit. After each fight I had to open her up wide and overtake the bomber and her convoy.

The cruising speed of these pursuit ships is around five hundred miles an hour, but they have a top speed of almost six hundred miles. The bombers cruise at about five hundred, with a top speed around five hundred and fifty.

Of the two thousand light and heavy bombers that started out with the fleet on this raid, about eighteen hundred got through to Ergos; and there, believe me, the real fighting commenced. Thousands upon thousands of Kapar planes soared into the air, and our fleet was augmented by the arrival of the survivors of the dogfights that we had left behind.

As the bombers unloaded their heavy bombs we could first see the flames of the explosions and then, after what seemed a long while, the sound of the detonation would come to us from twelve miles below. Ships were falling all about us, ours and the Kapars. Bullets screamed about us, and it was during this phase of the engagement that I lost my remaining after cockpit gunner.

Suddenly the Kapar fleet disappeared, and then the antiaircraft guns opened up on us. Like the antiaircraft guns of Unis, they fire a thousand-pound shell twelve or fifteen miles up into the air, and the burst scatters fragments of steel for five hundred yards in all directions. Other shells contain wire nets and small parachutes, which support the nets in the air to entangle and foul propellers.

After unloading our bombs, some seven or eight thousand tons of them, upon an area of two hundred square miles over and around Ergos, we started for home, circling to the east and then to the north, which would bring us in over the southernmost tip of Unis. I had two dead men in the after cockpit; and I hadn't been able to raise the gunner in the belly of the ship for some time; but as the ship had been hit many times, it was quite possible that the communicating system had been damaged. However, I feared that the man was dead.

As we circled over the eastern tip of Epris, my motor failed entirely, and there was nothing for me to do but come down. Another hour and I would have been within gliding distance of the tip of Unis, or one of the three islands which are an extension of this tip, at the southern end of the Karagan Ocean.

The crews of many ships saw me gliding down for a landing, but no ship followed to succor me. It is one of the rules of the service that other ships and men must not be jeopardized to assist a pilot who is forced down in enemy country. The poor devil is just written off as a loss, as he almost always needs to be.

I knew from my study of Polodian geography that I was beyond the southeastern boundary of Kapara, and over the country formerly known as Punos, one of the first to be subjugated by the Kapars over a hundred years before.

What the country was like I could only guess from rumors that are current in Unis, and which suggest that its people have been reduced to the status of wild beasts by years of persecution and starvation.

As I approached the ground I saw a mountainous country beneath me and two rivers which joined to form a very large river that emptied into a bay on the southern shoreline; but I found no people, no cities, and no indication of cultivated fields. Except along the river courses, where vegetation was discernible, the land appeared to be a vast wilderness. The whole terrain below me appeared pitted with ancient shell craters, attesting the terrific bombardment to which it had been subjected in a bygone day.

I had about given up all hope of finding a level place on which to make a landing, when I discovered one in the mouth of a broad canyon, at the southern foot of a range of mountains.

As I was about to set the ship down I saw figures moving a short distance up the canyon. At first I could not make out what they were, for they dodged behind trees in an evident effort to conceal themselves from me; but when the ship came to rest they came out, a dozen men armed with spears and bows and arrows. They wore loincloths made of the skins of some animal, and they carried long knives in their belts. Their hair was matted and their bodies were filthy and terribly emaciated.

They crept toward me, taking advantage of whatever cover the terrain afforded; and as they came they fitted arrows to their bows.

CHAPTER ELEVEN

THE ATTITUDE OF the reception committee was not encouraging. It seemed to indicate that I was not a welcome guest. I knew that if I let them get within bow range, a flight of arrows was almost certain to get me; so the thing to do was keep them out of bow range. I stood up in the cockpit and leveled my pistol at them, and they immediately disappeared behind rocks and trees.

I wished very much to examine my engine and determine if it were possible for me to repair it, but I realized that as long as these men of Punos were around that would be impossible. I might go after them; but they had the advantage of cover and of knowing the terrain; and while I might get some of them, I could not get them all; and those that I did not get would come back, and they could certainly hang around until after dark and then rush me.

It looked as though I were in a pretty bad way, but I finally decided to get down and go after them and have it out. Just then one of them stuck his head up above a rock and called to me. He spoke in one of the five languages of Unis that I had learned.

"Are you a Unisan?" he asked.

"Yes," I replied.

"Then do not shoot," he said. "We will not harm you."

"If that is true," I said, "go away."

"We want to talk to you," he said. "We want to know how the war is going and when it will end."

"One of you may come down," I said, "but not more."

"I will come," he said, "but you need not fear us."

He came down toward me then, an old man with wrinkled skin and a huge abdomen, which his skinny legs seemed scarcely able to support. His gray hair was matted with twigs and dirt, and he had the few gray hairs about his chin which connote old age on Poloda, where the men are beardless.

"I knew you were from Unis when I saw your blue uniform," he said. "In olden times the people of Unis and the people of Punos were good friends. That has been handed down from father to son for many generations. When the Kapars first attacked us, the men of Unis gave us aid; but they, too, were unprepared; and before they had the strength to help us we were entirely subjugated, and all of Punos was overrun with Kapars. They flew their ships from our coastlines, and they set up great guns there; but after a while the men of Unis built great fleets and drove them out. Then, however, it was too late for our people."

"How do you live?" I asked.

"It is hard," he said. "The Kapars still come over occasionally, and if they find a cultivated field they bomb and destroy it. They fly low and shoot any people they see, which makes it difficult to raise crops in open country; so we have been driven into the mountains, where we live on fish and roots and whatever else we can find.

"Many years ago," he continued, "the Kapars kept an army stationed here, and before they were through they killed every living thing that they could find—animals, birds, men, women, and children. Only a few hundred Punosans hid themselves in the inaccessible fastnesses of this mountain range, and in the years that have passed we have killed off all the remaining game for food faster than it could propagate."

"You have no meat at all?" I asked.

"Only when a Kapar is forced down near us," he replied.

"We hoped that you were a Kapar, but because you are a Unisan you are safe."

"But now that you are so helpless, why is it that the Kapars will not permit you to raise crops for food?"

"Because our ancestors resisted them when they invaded our country and that aroused the hatred upon which Kapars live. Because of this hatred they tried to exterminate us. Now they fear to let us get a start again, and if we were left alone there would be many of us in another hundred years; and once again we would constitute a menace to Kapara."

Harkas Yen had told me about Punos and I had also read something about the country in the history of Poloda. It had been inhabited by a virile and intelligent race of considerable culture. Its ships sailed the four great oceans of Poloda, carrying on commerce with the people of all the five continents. The central portion was a garden spot, supporting extensive farms, where grazed countless herds of livestock; and along its coastline were its manufacturing cities and its fisheries. I looked at the poor old devil standing before me: this, then, was what the warped, neurotic mind of one man could do to a happy and prosperous nation!

"Won't your ship fly?" he asked me.

"I don't know," I said. "I want to examine the motor and find out."

"You'd better let us push it into the canyon for you," he said. "It can be better hidden there from any Kapars who may fly over."

There was something about the poor old fellow that gave me confidence in him, and as the suggestion was a wise one, I accepted it. So he called his companions and they came down out of the canyon, eleven dirty, scrawny, hopeless-looking creatures of all ages. They tried to smile at me, but I guess the smiling muscles of their ancestors had commenced to atrophy generations before.

They helped me push the ship into the canyon, where, beneath a large tree, it was pretty well hidden from above.

I had forgotten the dead men aboard the ship; but one of the Punosans, climbing up on the wing, discovered the two in the after cockpit; and I knew that there must be another one in the belly of the ship. I shuddered as I thought what was passing through the creature's mind.

"There are dead men in the ship," he said to his fellows; and the old man, who was the leader, climbed up on the wing and looked; then he turned to me.

"Shall we bury your friends for you?" he asked, and a weight of fear and sorrow was lifted from my shoulders.

They helped me remove the cartridge belts and uniforms from the bodies of my friends and then they scooped out shallow graves with their knives and their hands, and laid the three bodies in them and covered them again.

When these sad and simple rites were ended, I started taking my engine down, the twelve Punosans hanging around and watching everything I did. They asked many questions about the progress of the war, but I could not encourage them to think that it would soon be over, or ever. They wanted to hear every detail of the battle I had just been in, and when I told them of the great numbers of Kapar ships that had been shot down, they were as pleased as children who have been told that they are going to a circus.

I found the damage that had been done to my engine, and I knew that I could make the necessary repairs, for we carried tools and spare parts; but it was getting late and soon it would be dark, so that I could not complete the repairs until the following day.

The old man realized this and asked me if I would come to their village and spend the night there. He said that it was a very poor village, and that there was not much food, but that I would be welcome because I had killed so many Kapars.

I could have slept in the ship, but purely out of curiosity I decided to accept his invitation.

Before we started for his village he touched me timidly on the arm. "May we have the guns and ammunition of your dead friends?" he asked. "If we had them, we might kill some more Kapars."

"Do you know how to use them?" I asked.

"Yes," he said, "we have found them on the bodies of Kapars who crashed here, and those whom we killed, but we have used up all the ammunition."

I didn't know what the authorities at Orvis would say about my giving away guns and ammunition. If these people could fight off and kill a few Kapars with them, it would not be a waste of material. When I told him that he might have them, he was so pleased that the tears came to his eyes when he tried to thank me, and he could not speak.

I followed them up the canyon and then along a narrow, precipitous trail that led to a tiny mesa on the shoulder of a towering peak. A waterfall tumbled from the cliff above into a little lake at its foot, and from there a mountain stream wandered across the mesa to leap over the edge of another cliff a mile away. Trees grew along one side of the stream and up to the foot of the cliff, and among these trees the village was hidden from the eyes of roving pilots.

Hide! Hide! Hide! A world in hiding. It seemed difficult to imagine that anyone had ever walked freely in the sunlight on the surface of Poloda without being ready to dodge beneath a tree, or into a hole in the ground; and I wondered if my world would ever come to that. It didn't seem possible; but for thousands of years, up until a hundred years ago, no inhabitant of Poloda would have thought it possible here.

In the village were a hundred people, forty women, fifty men, and ten children, poor, scrawny little things, with spindly arms and legs and enormous bellies, the result of stuffing themselves with grasses and twigs and leaves to assuage the pangs of hunger. When the villagers saw my escort coming in with me they ran forward hungrily, but when they recognized my blue uniform they stopped.

"He is our friend and guest," said the chief. "He has killed many Kapars, and he has given us guns and ammunition to kill more." And he showed them the weapons and the ammunition belts.

They crowded around me then and, like the twelve men, asked innumerable questions. They dwelt much upon the food we had in Unis, and were surprised to know that we had plenty to eat, for they thought that the Kapars must have devastated Unis as they had Punos.

The little children came timidly and felt of me. To them I was a man from another world. To me they were the indictment of a hideous regime.

The hunting party whose activities I had interrupted had brought in a couple of small rodents and a little bird. The women built a fire and put a large pot on it, in which there was a little water. Then they took the feathers off the bird and skinned the rodents, and threw them in without cleaning them. To this they added herbs and roots and handfuls of grass.

"The skins will make a little soup for the children for breakfast," an old woman explained to me as she laid them carefully aside.

They stirred the horrible mess with a piece of a small branch of a tree, and when it boiled the children clustered around to sniff the steam as it arose; and the adults formed a circle and stared at the pot hungrily.

I had never seen starving people before, and I prayed to God that I might never see any again unless I had the means wherewith to fill their bellies; and as I watched them I did not wonder that they ate Kapars, and I marveled at the kindliness and strength of will that kept them from eating me. When those mothers looked at me I could imagine that they were thinking of me in terms of steaks and chops which they must forgo although their children were starving.

In a community in which there were forty adult women there were only ten children, but I wondered how there could be any, as infant mortality must certainly be high among a starving people. I could imagine that I was looking at the remnant of a race that would soon be extinct, and I thought that there must be something wrong with all the religions in the universe that such a thing could happen to these people while the Kapars lived, and ate, and bred.

When they thought the mess in the pot was sufficiently cooked, little cups of clay, crudely burnt, were passed out, and the chief carefully measured out the contents of the pot with a large wooden ladle. When he came to me, I shook my head; and he looked offended.

"Is our fare too mean for you?" he asked.

"It is not that," I said; "I am well fed, and tomorrow I shall eat again. Here are starving men, and starving women, and, above all, starving children."

"Forgive me," he said. "You are a very kind man. The children shall have your share." Then he dipped out another cupful and divided it among the ten children, scarcely a mouthful apiece; but they were so grateful that once again the tears came to my eyes. I must be getting to be a regular softy; but before I came to Poloda I had never seen such sadness, such courage, such fortitude, or such suffering, as I have upon this poor war-torn planet.

CHAPTER TWELVE

NEXT MORNING the whole village accompanied me down the canyon to see me take off for Orvis. Three men went far in advance and when we got down into the canyon one of them came running back to meet us. I could see that he was very much excited, and he was motioning to us to be silent.

"There is a Kapar at your ship," he said, in a tremulous whisper.

"Let me go ahead," I said to the chief. "There will probably be shooting."

"We should have brought the guns," he said. "Why did I not think of that?" And he sent three men scurrying back to get them.

I walked down the canyon until I came to the other two men who had gone ahead. They were hiding behind bushes and they motioned me to take cover, but I had no time for that; and instead I ran forward, and when I came in sight of the ship a man was just climbing up onto the wing. He was a Kapar all right, and I started firing as I ran toward him. I missed him, and he wheeled about and held both hands above his head in sign of surrender.

I kept him covered as I walked toward him, but as I got nearer I saw that he was unarmed.

"What are you doing there, Kapar?" I demanded.

He came toward me, his hands still above his head.

"For the honor and glory of Unis," he said. "I am no Kapar." He removed his gray helmet, revealing a head of blond hair. But I had been told that there were some blond Kapars, and I was not to be taken in by any ruse.

"You'll have to do better than that," I said. "If you are a Unisan, you can prove it more convincingly than by showing a head of blond hair. Who are you, and from what city do you come?"

"I am Balzo Jan," he said, "and I come from the city of Orvis."

Now Balzo Jan was the brother that Balzo Maro had said was shot down in battle. This might be he, but I was still unconvinced.

"How did you get here?" I demanded.

"I was shot down in battle about two hundred miles from here," he said. "We made a good landing and some Kapars who saw that we were evidently not killed came down to finish us off. There were four of them and three of us. We got all four of them, but not before my two companions were killed. Knowing that I was somewhere in Epris, and therefore in Kapar-dominated country, I took the uniform of one of the Kapars as a disguise."

"Why didn't you take his gun and ammunition, too?"

"Because we had all exhausted all our ammunition," he replied, "and guns without ammunition are only an extra burden to carry. I had killed the last Kapar with my last bullet."

"You may be all right," I said, "but I don't know. Can you tell me the name of some of your sister's friends?"

"Certainly," he said. "Her best friends are Harkas Yamoda and Harkas Don, daughter and son of Harkas Yen."

"I guess you're all right," I said. "There are a couple of blue uniforms in the after cockpit. Get into one of them at once, and then we'll go to work on the motor."

"Look," he cried, pointing beyond me, "some men are coming. They are going to attack us."

I turned to see my friendly hosts creeping toward us with shafts fitted to their bows. Then I realized that they had seen the Kapar uniform, and I knew what was in their minds.

"It is all right," I shouted to them, "this is a friend."

"If he is a friend of yours, then you must be a Kapar," replied the chief.

"He is no Kapar," I insisted; and then I turned and shouted to Balzo Jan to get into a blue uniform as fast as he could.

"Perhaps you have deceived us," shouted the chief. "How do we know that you are not a Kapar, after all?"

"Our children are hungry," screamed a woman farther back up the canyon. "Our children are hungry, we are hungry, and here are two Kapars."

It was commencing to look very serious. The men were creeping closer; they would soon be within bow range. I had put my pistol back into its holster after I had been convinced that Balzo Jan was no impostor, and I did not draw it as I walked forward to meet the chief. He and his followers were surprised by this and didn't know what to do.

"We are friends," I said. "You see, I am not afraid of you. Would I have given you the three guns and the ammunition had I been a Kapar? Would I have let that man back there live if I had not known that he was a Unisan?"

The chief shook his head. "That is right," he said. "You would not have given us the guns and ammunition had you been a Kapar. But how do you know this man is not a Kapar?" he added suspiciously.

"Because he is the brother of a friend of mine," I explained. "He was shot down behind the Kapar lines and he took the uniform from a Kapar he had killed to use as a disguise, because he knew that he was in Kapar country."

About this time Balzo Jan crawled out of the after

cockpit dressed in the blue suit, boots, and helmet of a Unisan fighting man.

"Does he look like a Kapar?" I asked the chief.

"No," he said. "You must forgive us. My people hate the Kapars, and they are hungry."

With Balzo Jan's help I had the engine repaired and we were ready to take off a little after noon; and when we rose into the air the starving villagers stood sad-eyed and mute, watching us fly away toward a land of plenty.

As we rose above the mountains that lay between us and the coast I saw three ships far to our left. They were flying in a southwesterly direction toward Kapara.

"I think they are Kapars," said Balzo Jan, who was far more familiar with the lines of Polodian ships than I, having spent most of his lifetime looking at them.

Even as we watched, the three ships turned in our direction. Whatever they were, they had sighted us and were coming for us.

If they were Unisans, we had nothing to fear; nor for that matter did we have anything to fear if they were Kapars, for my ship could outfly them by a hundred miles an hour. Had they been as fast as ours, they could have cut us off, for they were in the right position to do so. We had been making about four hundred miles an hour and now I opened the throttle wide, for I did not purpose taking any chances, as I felt that we wouldn't have a chance against three Kapars, with three or four guns apiece, while we only had two. I opened the throttle, but nothing happened. The engine didn't accelerate at all. I told Balzo Jan.

"We shall have to fight, then," he said, "and I wanted to get home and get a decent meal. I have had practically nothing to eat for three days."

I knew how Balzo Jan felt, for I had had nothing to eat myself for some time, and anyway I had had enough fighting for a while.

"They are Kapars all right," said Balzo Jan presently.

There was no doubt about that now; the black of their wings and fuselages was quite apparent, and we were just about going to meet them over the islands off the southern tip of Unis. We were going to meet right over the last and largest of the three islands, which is called the Island of Despair, where are sent those confirmed criminals who are not to be destroyed, and those Unisans whose loyalty is suspected, but who cannot be convicted of treason.

I had been fiddling with the engine controls, trying to step up the speed a little, when the first burst of fire whistled about us. The leading ship was coming head-on toward us, firing only from her forward gun, when Balzo Jan sent a stream of explosive projectiles into her. I saw her propeller disappear then, and she started to glide toward the Island of Despair.

"That's the end of them," shouted Balzo Jan.

Quite suddenly and unexpectedly my motor took hold again, and we immediately drew away from the other two ships, which Balzo Jan was spraying with gunfire.

We must have been hit fifty times, but the plastic of our fuselage and wings could withstand machine-gun fire, which could injure us only by a lucky hit of propeller or instrument board. It is the heavier guns of combat planes and bombers that these fast, lightly armed pursuit planes have to fear.

"I hate to run from Kapars," I shouted back to Balzo Jan. "Shall we stay and have it out with them?"

"We have no right to throw away a ship and two men," he said, "in a hopeless fight."

Well, that was that. Balzo Jan knew the rules of the game better than I; so I opened the throttle wide and soon left the remaining Kapars far behind, and shortly after, they turned and resumed their flight toward Kapara.

There are two pilot seats and controls in the front cockpit, as well as the additional controls in the after cockpit. However, two men are seldom seated in the front cockpit, except for training purposes, as there is only one gun there and the Unisan military chiefs don't believe in wasting manpower. However, the seat was there, and I asked Balzo Jan to come up and sit with me.

"If you see any more Kapars," I said, "you can go back to your gun."

"Do you know," he said, after he had crawled up into the forward cockpit and seated himself beside me, "that we have been so busy since you first discovered me climbing into your ship that I haven't had a chance to ask you who you are. I know a lot of men in the fighting service, but I don't recall ever having seen you before."

"My name is Tangor," I said.

"Oh," he said, "you're the man that my sister discovered without any clothes on after a raid several months ago."

"The same," I said, "and she is mourning you for dead. I saw her at the Harkases the night before we took off for this last raid."

"My sister would not mourn," he said proudly.

"Well, she was mourning inwardly," I replied, "and sometimes that's worse for a woman than letting herself go. I should think a good cry now and then would be a relief to the women of Poloda."

"I guess they used to cry," he said, "but they don't anymore. If they cried every time they felt like crying, they'd be crying all the time; and they can't do that, you know, for there is work to do. It is war."

CHAPTER THIRTEEN

IT IS WAR! That was the answer to everything. It governed their every activity, their every thought. From birth to death they knew nothing but war. Their every activity was directed at the one purpose of making their country more fit for war.

"I should think you would hate war," I said to Balzo Jan.

He looked at me in surprise. "Why?" he demanded. What would we do with ourselves if there were no war?"

"But the women," I said. "What of them?"

"Yes," he replied, "it is hard on them. The men only have to die once, but the women have to suffer always. Yes; it is too bad; but I can't imagine what we would do without war."

"You could come out in the sunshine, for one thing," I said, "and you could rebuild your cities, and devote some of your time to cultural pursuits and to pleasure. You could trade with other countries, and you could travel to them; and wherever you went you would find friends."

Balzo Jan looked at me skeptically. "Is that true in your world?" he asked.

"Well, not when I was last there," I had to admit, "but then, several of the countries were at war."

"You see," he said, "war is the natural state of man, no matter what world he lives in."

We were over the southern tip of Unis now. The majestic peaks of the Mountains of Loras were at our left, and at our right the great river which rises in the mountains south of Orvis emptied into the sea, fifteen hundred miles from its source. It is a mighty river, comparable, I should say, to the Amazon. The country below us was beautiful in the extreme, showing few effects of the war, for they have many buried cities here whose Labor Corps immediately erase all signs of the devastating effects of Kapar raids as soon as the enemy has departed.

Green fields stretched below us in every direction, attesting the fact that agriculture on the surface still held its own against the Kapars on this part of the continent; but I knew at what a price they raised their crops with low-flying Kapar planes strafing them with persistent regularity, and bombers blasting great craters in their fields.

But from high above this looked like heaven to me, and I wondered if it were indeed for me the locale of that afterlife which so many millions of the people of my world hope and pray for. It seemed to me entirely possible that my transition to another world was not unique, for in all the vast universe there must be billions of planets, so far removed from the ken of Earth men that their existence can never be known to them.

I mentioned to Balzo Jan what was passing in my mind and he said, "Our people who lived before the war had a religion, which taught that those who died moved to Uvala, one of the planets of our solar system which lies upon the other side of Omos. But now we have no time for religion; we have time only for war."

"You don't believe in a life hereafter, then?" I asked.

"Well, I didn't either, once, but I do now."

"Is it really true that you come from another world?" he asked. "Is it true that you died there and came to life again on Poloda?"

"I only know that I was shot down by an enemy plane behind the enemy lines," I replied. "A machine-gun bullet struck me in the heart, and during the fifteen seconds that consciousness remained I remember losing control of my ship and going into a spin. A man with a bullet in his heart, spinning toward the ground from an altitude of ten thousand feet, must have died."

"I should think so," said Balzo Jan, "but how did you get here?"

I shrugged. "I don't know any more about it than you do," I replied. "Sometimes I think it is all a dream from which I must awake."

He shook his head. "Maybe you are dreaming," he said, "but I am not. I am here, and I know that you are here with me. You may be a dead man, but you seem very much alive to me. How did it seem to die?"

"Not bad at all," I replied. "I only had fifteen seconds to think about it, but I know that I died happy because I had shot down two of the three enemy planes that had attacked me."

"Life is peculiar," he said. "Because you were shot down in a war on a world countless millions of miles away from Poloda, I am now alive and safe. I can't help but be glad, my friend, that you were shot down."

It was a quiet day over Unis; we reached the mountains south of Orvis without sighting a single enemy plane, and after crossing the mountains I dropped to within about a hundred feet of the ground. I like to fly low when I can; it breaks the monotony of long flights, and we ordinarily fly at such tremendous altitudes here that we see very little of the terrain.

As we dropped down I saw something golden glinting in the sunshine below us. "What do you suppose that is down there?" I said to Balzo Jan, banking so that he could see it.

"I don't know," he said, "but it looks amazingly like a woman lying there; but what a woman would be lying out in the open for, so far from the city, I can't imagine."

"I am going down to see," I said.

I spiraled down and as we circled over the figure I saw

that it was indeed a woman, lying upon her face—an unmarried woman, I knew, for her suit was of golden sequins. She lay very still, as though she were asleep.

I put the plane down and taxied up close to her. "You stay at the controls, Balzo Jan," I said, for one must always think of Kapars and be ready to run, or fight, or hide.

I dropped to the ground and walked over to the still form. The girl's helmet had fallen off, and her mass of copper-red hair spread over and hid that part of her face which was turned up. I knelt beside her and turned her over, and as I saw her face my heart leaped to my throat—it was Harkas Yamoda, little Harkas Yamoda, crushed and broken.

There was blood on her lips, and I thought she was dead; but I didn't want to believe it, I wouldn't believe it; and so I placed my ear against her breast and listened—and faintly I heard the beating of her heart. I lifted the little form in my arms, then, and carried it to the ship.

"It is Harkas Yamoda," I said to Balzo Jan, as I passed her up to him; "she is still alive. Put her in the after cockpit." Then I sprang to the wing of the ship and told Balzo Jan to take the controls and bring the ship in.

I got in with Harkas Yamoda and held her in my arms as gently as I could, while the ship bumped over the rough ground during the takeoff. I wiped the blood from her lips; that was all I could do, that and pray. I had not prayed before since I was a little boy at my mother's knee. I remember wondering, if there were a God, if He could hear me, so very far away, for I had always thought of God as being somewhere up in our own heaven.

It was only a matter of fifteen or twenty minutes before Balzo Jan set the ship down outside of Orvis and taxied down the ramp to our underground airdrome.

There are always fleets of ambulances at every airdrome, for there are always wounded men in many of the ships that come in. Also, close by is an emergency hospital; and to this I drove with Harkas Yamoda, after telling Balzo Jan to notify her father.

The surgeons worked over her while I paced the floor outside. They worked very quickly and she had only just been carried to her room when Harkas Yen, and Don, and Yamoda's mother came. The four of us stood around that silent, unconscious little form lying so quietly on her cot.

"Have you any idea how it happened?" I asked Harkas Yen.

He nodded. "Yes," he said, "she was on an outing with some of her friends when they were attacked by Kapars. The men put up a good fight and several of them were killed. The girls ran, but a Kapar overtook Yamoda and carried her away."

"She must have jumped from the plane," said Don.

"Planes!" said Yamoda's mother bitterly. "Planes! The curse of the world. History tells us that when they were first perfected and men first flew in the air over Poloda, there was great rejoicing, and the men who perfected them were heaped with honors. They were to bring the peoples of the world closer together. They were to break down international barriers of fear and suspicion. They were to revolutionize society by bringing all peoples together, to make a better and happier world in which to live. Through them civilization was to be advanced hundreds of years; and what have they done? They have blasted civilization from nine-tenths of Poloda and stopped its advance in the other tenth. They have destroyed a hundred thousand cities and millions of people, and they have driven those who have survived underground, to live the lives of burrowing rodents. Planes! The curse of all times. I hate them. They have taken thirteen of my sons, and now they have taken my daughter."

"It is war," said Harkas Yen, with bowed head.

"This is not war," cried the sad-faced woman, pointing at the still form upon the cot.

"No," I said, "this is not war—it is rapine and murder."

"What else can you expect of the Kapars?" demanded Harkas Don. "But for this they shall pay."

"For this they shall pay," I, too, swore.

Then the surgeons came in and we looked at them questioningly. The senior surgeon put his hand on the shoulder of Yamoda's mother and smiled. "She will live," he said. "She was not badly injured."

Yes; planes used in war are a curse to humankind, but thanks to a plane Balzo Maro's brother had been returned to her, and little Yamoda would live.

Listen! The sirens are sounding the general alarm.

Editor's Note: I have sat before my typewriter at midnight many a night since that last line was typed by unseen hands. I have wondered if Tangor ever came back from the battle to which that general alarm called him, or if he died a second death. I am still wondering.

PART II

TANGOR RETURNS

FOREWORD

NATURALLY, MY IMAGINATION has been constantly intrigued by speculation as to the fate of Tangor, since his unseen, perhaps ghostly, fingers typed the story of his advent upon Poloda, that mysterious planet some 450,000 light-years from Earth; typed them upon my own machine one midnight while I sat amazed, incredulous, and fascinated, with my hands folded in my lap.

His story told of his death behind the German lines in September 1939, when he was shot down in a battle with three Messerschmitts, and of how he had found himself, alive, uninjured, and as naked as the day he was born, in another world.

I hung upon every line that he wrote; his description of the underground city of Orvis with its great buildings that were lowered deep beneath the surface of the ground when the Kapar bombers flew over by thousands to drop their lethal bombs in the great war that has already lasted more than a hundred years.

I followed his adventures after he became a flier in the air corps of Unis, the Polodian country of his adoption. I grieved with him at the bedside of little Harkas Yamoda; and there were tears of relief in my eyes, as there must have been in his, when the surgeons announced that she would live.

And then the last line that he typed: "Listen! The sirens are sounding the general alarm."

That was all. But I have sat before my typewriter at midnight many a night since that last line was typed by unseen hands. I have wondered if Tangor ever came back from the battle to which that general alarm called him, or if he died a second death and, perhaps, a final one.

I had about given up my midnight vigils as useless, when one night recently, shortly before midnight, I was awakened by a hand upon my shoulder. It was a moonlight night. The objects in the room were faintly visible, yet I could see no one. I switched on the reading light at the head of my bed. Other than myself there was no one in the room, or at least no one I could see; and then I heard and saw the space bar of my typewriter moving up and down with something that seemed like a note of urgency.

As I started to get out of bed, I saw a sheet of typewriter paper rise from my desk as though endowed with life and place itself in the typewriter. By the time I reached my desk and sat down before the machine, those ghostly fingers had already started to type the story which you are about to read.

Tangor had returned!

CHAPTER ONE

THAT GENERAL ALARM certainly called us to a real battle. The Kapars sent over ten thousand planes, and we met them over the Bay of Hagar with fully twenty thousand. Perhaps a thousand of them got through our lines to drop their bombs over Orvis, those that our pursuit planes did not overtake and shoot down; but we drove the others out over the Karagan Ocean, into which ships plunged by the thousands.

At last they turned and fled for home, but we pursued them all the way to Ergos, flying low over the very city, strafing them as they taxied for their ramps; then we turned back, perhaps ten thousand ships out of the twenty thousand that had flown out to meet the Kapars. We had lost ten thousand ships and perhaps fifty thousand men, but we had practically annihilated the Kapar fleet and had saved Unis from a terrific bombing; and on the way back, we met a few straggling Kapars returning, shooting down every last one of them.

Once more all three of my gunners were killed, while I came through without a scratch. Either I have a charmed life or else, having died once, I cannot die again.

I saw practically nothing of Harkas Yamoda while she was convalescing, as the doctors had ordered that she have perfect rest; but a flier has to have relaxation, and he has to have girl friends—he sees altogether too much of men while he is on duty, as about half of those he does see are firing rifles or machine guns or cannons at him. It is a nerve-racking business, and the majority of us are always on edge most of the time when we are on the ground. It is a strange thing; but that restlessness and nervousness seem to leave me when I am in the air; and of course when you are in battle, you haven't time to think of such things.

There was a girl working in the office of the Commissioner for War, whom I had seen and talked to many times. She was always exceedingly pleasant to me and as she seemed a nice sort, intelligent and witty, I finally asked her to have dinner with me.

We had a pleasant evening together, and after that I saw a great deal of her when I was off duty. She liked to get me to talk about my own world, way off there so far beyond Canapa.

Once, after we had been going together for some time, Morga Sagra said she couldn't understand why it was I was so loyal to Unis when I hadn't been born there and had no relations, even, on the planet.

"Suppose you had come down in Kapara," she asked, "instead of in Unis?"

I shrugged. "I don't like to think of it," I said; "I am sure that I never could have fought for and been loyal to the Kapars."

"What do you know about them," she asked, "except what we Unisans have told you? and naturally, we are biased. As a matter of fact, I don't think they are a bad sort at all, and their form of government is based upon a much more enduring concept than ours."

"Just what do you mean?" I asked.

"It is based on war," said Morga Sagra, "and war is the natural state of the human race. War is their way of life. They are not always thinking of peace as are we."

"You wouldn't like peace?" I asked.

"No!" she exclaimed, "I should hate it. Think of having to associate with men who never fought. It would be disgusting. If I were a man, I would join the Kapars, for they are going to win the war eventually."

"That is a very dangerous thing to say, Morga Sagra," I told her.

"I'm not afraid to tell you," she said; "you are no Unisan, you owe no more allegiance to Unis than you do to Kapara. Listen, Tangor; don't be stupid. You are an alien here; you have made a good record as a fighter, but what can it get you?—nothing. You will always be an alien, who can do no more than fight for Unis—and probably get killed in the long run."

"Well, and what do you want me to do, stop fighting?"

"No," she said, leaning close to me and whispering; "I want you to go to Kapara and take me with you. You and I could go far there with the Unisan military secrets we could take with us."

I was immeasurably shocked, but I did not let her see it. The little fool was a traitor, and if she had thought that I was greatly shocked by what she had said, she would be afraid that I might turn her in to the authorities. If she would turn against Unis for no reason whatsoever other than a perverted admiration for the Kapars, she certainly wouldn't hesitate to turn against me if she had reason to fear me. She was right, I am an alien here. Any lie that she could make up might be believed.

"You take me by surprise, Morga Sagra," I said; "I had never thought of such a thing. I don't believe that it could be done; the Kapars would never accept me."

After that she evidently thought that I could be won over easily, for she told me that she had long been in touch with Kapar sympathizers in Orvis and knew two Kapar secret agents well.

"I have discussed this matter with them," she said, "and they have promised me that you and I will be treated like kings of old if we can get to Ergos. That's the capital of Kapara," she added.

"Yes, I know," I told her; "I have been there."

"You have!" she exclaimed.

"Yes, to drop bombs on it. It would be amusing to go there now to live, and have my old comrades in arms dropping bombs on me."

"Then you'll go?" she asked.

"Let me think it over, Morga Sagra," I said; "this is not something that a man can do without thought."

So we left it that way, and the next day I went to the Commissioner for War and told him the whole story, and I didn't have even a single qualm of conscience for betraying Morga Sagra; she was a traitor and she tried to make a traitor of me. While I am on Poloda, Unis will be as dear to me as my own United States of America. I wear the uniform of her fighting force; I have been well treated; my friends are here; they trust me, as do my superiors and my fellow fighters. I could never betray them.

The Commissioner for War is a crusty old fellow, and he almost blew up like one of his own bombs when he learned that a Kapar agent was employed in his department.

"She'll be shot tomorrow!" he exploded, and then he thought a moment and calmed down. "Maybe it would be better to let her live," he said; "maybe we can use her. Come with me."

He took me to the Eljanhai's office and there he had me repeat what I had told him. "It is too bad," said the Eljanhai; "I knew her father well; he was a brave officer. He was killed in battle when she was a little baby. I hate to think of ordering his daughter destroyed, but I suppose there is no other way."

"I have another way," said the Commissioner for War. "I suggest that if Tangor will accept the mission, we let him accede to Morga Sagra's proposition. As you know, the Kapars are supposed to have perfected a power amplifier which will permit them to fly to great distances from Poloda, possibly to other planets. I have heard you say that you wished that we could get the drawings of this new amplifier." He turned to me. "It would be a very dangerous mission, Tangor, and one in which you might not possibly be able to succeed, but there would be a chance, if you were there. What do you say to it?"

"I am in the service of Unis," I said; "whatever you wish me to do, I will do to the best of my ability."

"Excellent," said the Eljanhai, "but do you realize that the chances are about a thousand to one that you will be unsuccessful and that you will never get out of Kapara alive."

"I realize that, sir," I said, "but I take similar chances almost every day of my life."

"Then it is settled," he said; "let us know when you are ready to go, and every arrangement will be made to facilitate your departure; and, by the way, when you get to Kapara, see if you can get any information as to the fate of one of our most valuable secret agents from whom we have not heard for two years; he is an officer named Handon Gar," and then he described the man very minutely to me, as I could not, of course, inquire about him, and furthermore, he had unquestionably changed his name after he reached Kapara.

The two then gave me certain military information to report to the Kapars, information they were perfectly willing to trade for a chance to get the secret of the amplifier.

I wondered just why they were so anxious to obtain the secret of this power amplifier and so I made bold to ask.

"To be perfectly frank," said the Eljanhai, "Unis is tired of war; and we wish to send an expedition to one of the nearer planets, either Tonos or Antos, to see what conditions are there; and if they are better, eventually to transport all Unisans to one of these planets."

What an amazing and stupendous project, it was staggering even to contemplate—an heroic migration unparalleled in history.

"But if you get the secret," warned the Eljanhai, "you must destroy all copies of the plans you do not bring away with you, and destroy also all those who could reproduce them, so that the Kapars cannot follow. Our sole desire is to find some world free from war, and no world would be free from war if there were Kapars there."

I saw Morga Sagra again that evening. "Well," she asked, "have you made up your mind?"

"Yes," I replied. "I have come to the conclusion that you were right; I owe these people nothing, and if the Kapars are going to win this war, I might as well be on the winning side."

"You are quite right," she said; "you will never regret it. I have made all the necessary arrangements for our entry into Kapara, but the problem of getting out of Unis is for you to solve."

"I will take care of everything," I told her, "and in the meantime I think that we should not be seen together too much. Hold yourself in readiness to leave at any moment; I may call for you tomorrow or the next day."

We parted then and I went out to the Harkases' to bid them good-bye. Yamoda was stronger and had been moved out into the garden, where she lay on a couch in the artificial sunlight which illuminates this underground city. She seemed so genuinely happy to see me that I hated to tell her that I was going away for an indefinite period. We had become such excellent friends that it saddened us both to realize that we might not see one another again for a considerable time, and her lip trembled when I told her that I had come to say good-bye. She seemed to sense that this was more than an ordinary parting to which the women of Unis are so accustomed.

"How long will you be gone?" she asked.

"I have no idea," I replied.

"Then I suppose that you can't tell me where you are going, either."

"No, I can't," I replied; "about all I can tell you is that it is a secret mission."

She nodded and placed her hand on mine. "You will be careful of yourself, won't you, Tangor?" she asked.

"Yes, Yamoda, I will be careful; and I will try to get back as quickly as possible, for I shall miss you very much."

"You have been doing very well without me lately," she said, with a mischievous twinkle in her eye; "is she such very good company?"

"She is better than nobody," I replied, "and I get terribly lonesome when I can't come out here."

"I don't believe I know her," she said; "she does not go with the same people I do."

I thought I noticed just a trace of contemptuousness in that speech, something quite unlike Yamoda. "I have never met any of her friends," I said. Just then Yamoda's mother came into the garden, and we talked of other things. They insisted on my staying to dinner.

When I left, later in the evening, it was very hard for me to say good-bye to them all, for the Harkases are my best friends in Unis, and Don and Yamoda are just like brother and sister to me; in fact their mother calls me her other son.

CHAPTER TWO

EARLY THAT FOLLOWING morning, I called on the Commissioner for War, and told him that I planned on leaving that day. I explained in detail the procedure I wished to follow to get Morga Sagra out of Orvis, and he told me that everything would be arranged in accordance with my plans. He then gave me a sheaf of military documents which I was to turn over to the Kapars as proof of my good faith and of my potential value to them.

"You will need something to meet expenses while you are there," he said, and he handed me a heavy leather pouch. "As there is no longer any monetary medium of international exchange," he continued, "you will have to do the best you can with the contents of this pouch, which contains gold and precious stones. I shall immediately instruct your squadron commander that you have been ordered to make a reconnaissance flight alone and that the mission is a secret one; he is to see that no one is in the hangar between the third and fourth hours after noon, as it is my wish that no one sees you depart. During that time, you can smuggle in your coconspirator; and now good-bye, my boy, and good luck. The chances are that I shall never see you again, but I shall remember you as one who died gloriously for the honor and glory of Unis."

That sounded altogether too much like an obituary, and I went away thinking of the little white cross somewhere in the Rhine Valley. If what I had been told about the Kapars were true, I would have no little white cross there, as my body would be shipped off to serve as food for some of their subjugated peoples working in slavery for them.

I called on Sagra at the third hour after noon. "Everything is arranged," I told her, "and we shall be on our way within the hour."

She had not smiled as she usually did when we met, and I noticed a certain constraint in her manner. Finally the cause of it came out, as she blurted, "What were you doing in conference with the Commissioner for War this morning?"

"How did you think I was going to get out of Orvis?" I demanded. "I had to work on the old chap a long time to get him to order me to make a reconnaissance flight alone."

"I'm sorry," she said, "but this is dangerous business; and when one's life is constantly at stake, suspicion becomes almost an obsession."

"I can well understand that," I said; "but if our mission is to be successful, we must trust one another fully."

"I shan't doubt you again," she said, "but right now my nerves are on edge. I am really terrified, for I don't see how you are going to get me out of the city; and if you are caught trying it, we'll both be shot."

"Don't worry," I said; "just do as I tell you."

We went out to my car then, and I had her get in the rear compartment, and when I was sure that no one was looking, I told her to lie down on the floor; then I threw an old robe over her.

I drove directly to the hangar, which I found entirely deserted. I drove as close to my ship as I could and then had Sagra crawl into the gunner's compartment in the belly of the fuselage. A moment later I had taxied up the ramp and taken off.

"Which way?" I asked Sagra, over the communicating system.

"Northwest," she replied. "When can I get out of here? I don't like it down here."

"In just a moment," I replied.

By mutual agreement, Sagra had kept all of the plans covering our flight to Kapara and our entry into that country to herself. My job had been to simply get the military secrets and get us out of Orvis.

A small hatchway in the ceiling of the compartment in which Sagra was led to the rear gunner's cockpit, and when I told her to come up with me, she came through this hatchway and climbed over into the forward cockpit.

"Now," I said, "you can tell me why we are flying northwest if we are going to Kapara, which lies southwest of Unis."

"It's a long way around, I know," she said, "but it's the only way in which we can eventually enter Kapara in a Kapar plane. In this plane and with that uniform of yours, we'd not get far in Kapara; so we are flying to Gorvas first."

Gorvas is a city on the continent of Karis, the farthest removed from the continent of Epris on which Kapara is situated. It is a poor barren continent, and the one least affected by the war, for it possesses nothing that the Kapars want.

After an uneventful flight, we landed at Gorvas. No fighting planes had come up to meet us, and no antiaircraft shells had burst around us, as we had circled above Gorvas before landing; for the people of Karis know they have nothing to fear from Unis, and we received a friendly greeting from some officers at the airport.

Morga Sagra had obtained forged credentials for us, and she had told me that my name hereafter would be Korvan Don, while she would keep her own name which was favorably known to her connections in Ergos, the capital of Kapara.

After leaving the airport, Sagra told the driver of the public conveyance we had hired to drive to a certain house, the address of which had been given her by a Kapar agent in Orvis.

Gorvas is a poor city, but at least it is not underground, although, as I was told, every building has its bombproof cellar. Occasionally we saw bomb craters, indicating that the Kapars came even here to this faraway, barren country, either because the Kerisans were known to be friendly with Unis or just to satisfy their inordinate lust for destruction.

Our driver took us to a poor part of town and stopped before a mean little one-story stone house where we dismissed him. We stood there until he had driven away; then Sagra led the way along the street to the third house, after which she crossed the street to the house directly opposite. It was all quite mysterious, but it showed the care with which everything had been arranged to avoid leaving a well-marked trail.

Approaching the door of this house, which was a little more pretentious than the one before which we had first stopped, Sagra knocked three times in rapid succession, and then twice more at intervals; and after a moment the door was opened by a hard-faced, scowling man.

"What do you want?" he demanded gruffly.

"I am Morga Sagra," replied my companion, "and this is Korvan Don."

"Come in," said the man; "I've been expecting you. Let me see your credentials."

Sagra handed him a perfectly blank piece of paper. I was standing near the man, and when he opened it up, I saw that there was nothing on it.

"Sit down," said the man, and then he went to a desk; and, seating himself there, took what appeared to be a pocket flashlight from one of the drawers and shone its light upon the paper.

The light must have made writing on the paper visible for I could see him passing it back and forth and that his eyes followed it. Presently he got up and handed the paper back to Sagra.

"You will remain here," he said, "while I go and complete arrangements." Then he left us.

"Do you know that fellow's name?" I asked Sagra.

"Yes," she said.

"What is it? Why didn't you introduce me?"

"His name is none of your business," said Sagra. "You must learn not to ask questions, Korvan Don; however, just to satisfy your curiosity, I don't mind telling you that his name is Gompth."

"What a beautiful name," I said, "but as far as I am concerned you needn't have told me what it was. His name doesn't interest me any more than his face."

"Don't say things like that," snapped Sagra. "He is a very important person, and it is not wise to make unpleasant remarks about important persons. Now be sure not to let him know that you know his name, for that is not the name that he goes by here."

I was getting my introduction to the fear and suspicion which hangs like a pall over everything Kaparan. I had said that I did not care whether I knew this man's name or not, for how could I know that one day I should be very glad that I did know it.

In about an hour, Gompth returned. He had brought with him civilian clothing such as is worn by the inhabitants of Karis, and after we had changed into it, he drove us out into the country, where he turned an old Karisan plane over to us.

It was not until Sagra and I were in the plane that he gave us our final instructions, and handed us credentials. He directed us to fly to a city called Pud, on the continent of Auris, and report to a man with the poetic name of Frink.

"What will become of my plane?" I asked him.

"What difference does it make to you?" he demanded.

"It makes a great deal of difference to me," I snapped,

for I was getting fed up with all this rudeness and secrecy. "I expect that, unquestionably, I shall be sent on missions to Unis; and if I am, I shall need my plane and my uniform."

He eyed me suspiciously before he replied. "How could you ever return to Unis without being destroyed as a traitor?" he asked.

"Because I used my head before I left Orvis," I replied; "I arranged to be sent out on a reconnaissance flight, and I can think of a hundred excuses to explain even a long absence."

"If you ever need your plane or your uniform," he said, "they will be here when you return."

I breathed more freely when we rose into the clear air and left Mr. Gompth behind. His was a most depressing personality. His conversation gave the impression that he was snapping at you like an ill-natured dog, and not once while we were with him had he smiled. I wondered if all the Kapars were like that.

In Pud we found Frink by the same devious means that we had arrived at the house of Gompth, only here there was a slight difference; we were allowed to call Frink by name, because Frink was not his name.

We stayed overnight in Pud; and in the morning, Frink gave us Kapar clothes, and later furnished us with a Kapar plane, a very excellent plane too; and for that I was glad, as I had not been very happy crossing the Voldan Ocean from Karis to Auris in the ancient crate that Gompth had furnished us. Before us lay a flight of some two thousand miles across the Mandan Ocean from Auris to Kapara.

The crossing was monotonous and uneventful, but after we got over Kapara, and were winging toward Ergos, we sighted a squadron of Unisan planes that were doubtless on reconnaissance. I turned away in an effort to avoid them, but they took after us.

The ship I was piloting was a very swift scouting plane lightly armed. There was a bow gun which I could operate and one gun in an after cockpit, which Morga Sagra could not have operated even had I wished her to. I had no intention of firing on a Unisan plane under any circumstances, and so I turned and ran.

They chased me out across the Mandan Ocean for nearly a thousand miles before they gave up and turned back. I followed, keeping just within sight of them, until they bore to the south with the evident intention of passing around the southern end of the continent of Epris; then I opened the throttle wide and streaked for Ergos.

When we ran down a ramp into the city, we were immediately surrounded by men in green uniforms; and an officer gruffly demanded our credentials. I told him that our instructions were to hand them to Gurrul and then he bundled us into a car, and we were driven off, surrounded by green-clad members of the Zabo, the secret police of Kapara.

Ergos is a large city, sprawling around deep underground. We passed first through a considerable district in which there were indications of the direst poverty. The buildings were principally flimsy shelters and sometimes only holes in the ground, into which people scurried when they saw the green uniforms of the Zabo. But presently we came to more substantial buildings, which were all identical except in the matter of size. There was not the slightest indication of ornamentation on any of them. The ride was most uninteresting, just one monotonous mile after another until we approached the center of the city where the buildings suddenly became rococo in their ornateness.

The car stopped before one of the more hideous of these buildings, a multicolored atrocity, the facade of which was covered with carved figures and designs.

We were hustled out of the car and into the building, and a moment later we were ushered into the office of Gurrul, Chief of the Zabo, the most feared man in all Kapara.

CHAPTER THREE

GURRUL WAS A GROSS MAN with a cruel mouth and close-set eyes. He scrutinized us in silence for a full minute, as though he were trying to read our in-most thoughts. He was really fixing in his mind every detail of our appearance, and he would know us again whenever or wherever he saw us and only the cleverest of disguises could deceive him. It is said of him that Gurrul knows a million people thus, but that seems to me like an exaggeration.

He took our credentials and examined them carefully; then he asked for the military secrets I had brought from Orvis, and when I turned them over to him he glanced through them hurriedly, giving no indication of any great interest in them.

"You flew for the enemy?" he demanded of me.

"Yes," I replied.

"Why?" he asked.

"Because I knew no other country than Unis," I explained.

"Why did you turn against the country of your birth?" he asked.

"Unis is not the country of my birth."

"Where were you born?"

"On another planet in another solar system millions of miles from here."

He scowled at me fiercely and pounded his desk until everything on it danced. "You dare stand there and tell me such a lie, you fool!" he cried; "you, a filthy Unisan, dare insult my intelligence thus. Possibly you have never heard of Gurrul, you idiot. If you had, you would have cut your own throat before you came to him with such a story."

"Most High," said Morga Sagra timidly, "I believe that he speaks the truth—everyone in Orvis believes him."

He wheeled on her angrily. "Who told you to speak?" he snapped.

"Forgive me, Most High," she said. She was trembling all over, and I was afraid that her knees were going to give away beneath her.

Gurrul turned to one of his lieutenants. "Have them searched and then lock them up," he ordered, and that was the end of our reception in Kapara, where they were going to receive us with open arms and load us with honors.

My gold and jewels were taken from me, and Morga Sagra and I were locked up in a cell in the basement of the Zabo headquarters. Our cell was nothing but an iron cage, and I could see corridor after corridor of them closely packed together, and all of them appeared to have occupants, sometimes six or eight people jammed into a cage scarcely large enough for two.

Most of our fellow prisoners whom I could see sat dejectedly on the stone floor of their cages, their heads bowed upon their chests; but there were others who jibbered and screamed, those whom torture and confinement had driven mad. When the screaming annoyed a guard too much, he would come down to the cage and turn a hose upon the screaming inmate. From the first hour that we were there, for a solid hour, one of the poor creatures screamed incessantly. One guard after another turned the hose on him, but still he screamed. Finally the head keeper came in, an officer covered with gold braid, medals, and brass buttons. He walked up to the maniac's cage and deliberately shot him through the heart. He did it as casually as one might swat a fly, and then he walked away without a backward glance.

"You must be very happy," I said to Morga Sagra.

"What do you mean?" she whispered.

"You are in your beloved Kapara at last, surrounded by your dear friends."

"Hush," she cautioned, "someone will hear you."

"Why should I hush?" I asked. "Don't you want them to know how fond you are of them?"

"I am fond of them," she said; "this is all a terrible mistake, but it is your fault—you never should have told that story to Gurrul."

"You wouldn't want me to lie to the Most High, would you?"

"You must not use that tone of voice when you speak of anyone here," she whispered; "the first thing you know, you'll get us both beheaded."

We were kept in that vile hole for a week, and almost every waking hour we expected to be taken out and destroyed. Morga Sagra was virtually a nervous wreck when, at last, they did come for us.

Sagra was so weak from fright that the guards had to support her as we were led along a corridor. Finally one of them said to her, "You have nothing to fear; you are going to be released."

At that Sagra collapsed completely and sat down on the stone floor. The guards laughed and picked her up and practically carried her the rest of the way. They were still carrying her when I was hustled off down another corridor.

They took me from the building through a rear doorway and put me into what looked like a big green moving van. It was so filled with humanity that they had to push me in and then slammed the doors on me quickly before I fell out. There was an iron-barred window in front, and a guard with a rifle in his hand sat facing it.

As soon as the doors were closed and locked, the truck

started off, the human load swaying to and fro, trampling on each other's toes and cursing beneath its breath. That was a ride to be long remembered for its discomforts. The heat from the men's bodies became absolutely oppressive, and the air so foul that one could scarcely breathe.

The vehicle moved at a high rate of speed. How long we were in it, I do not know; but I should imagine about two hours, because it seemed like ten; but at last it stopped and turned around and was backed up to stop again. Then the doors were opened, and we were ordered out.

I saw before me a very large enclosure, surrounded by a high wire fence. There were open sheds along two sides. There were several hundred men in the enclosure, and they were all dressed alike in black clothes with big white numbers across the front and back. I didn't have to be told that I was in a prison camp.

There was sort of an office by the gate where we were taken from the truck, and here our names were entered in a book and we were given prison uniforms and numbers. Then we were ordered into the enclosure with the other prisoners. They were a filthy, emaciated lot with the most hopeless expressions I have ever seen on human faces. When I had been taken from my cell, I had felt that I was going to be beheaded, but I could conceive that this was infinitely worse.

I had asked the officer who had checked us in why I was being imprisoned and for how long, but he had just told me to shut up and speak only when I was spoken to.

This was a work camp, and when I say work that doesn't half describe it. We were usually employed on the hardest kind of manual labor for sixteen hours a day. There was one day of rest in every ten; it had been upon one of the rest days that I had arrived. There were both men and women in the camp, and they came from nearly every country of Poloda. We were treated just like animals, the prison clothes they gave us had to last a year, and we only had the one suit in which we worked and slept. Most of the men, and women too, were in nothing but rags. The food that was given us was indescribable. It was thrown into troughs twice a day just as food is given to hogs. Men and women both were insulted, beaten, kicked, often killed. We were not allowed to use names even among ourselves—just our numbers.

Day and night, guards patrolled just outside the wire fence; and if they saw prisoners talking, they yelled at them to stop and sometimes they came inside and beat them. Nevertheless we did talk, for it was hard to stop us after dark; and finally I made a few friends.

There was one who said that he came from Orvis, with whom I became quite friendly, although I knew it was dangerous, as the Kapars planted many spies in these camps. Finally, however, I came to the conclusion that this Tunzo Bor was all right, and so I asked him if he knew a man named Handon Gar.

Immediately he was all suspicion. "No," he said, "I don't know anyone by that name. Why do you ask?"

"I have a message for him," I replied.

"From whom?" he asked.

"From a friend in Orvis."

"Well, I don't know any Handon Gar," he insisted, "and if he is here you may rest assured he is not known by that name."

"I suppose not," I said, "but I certainly wish that I could find him, as I should like to deliver my message."

I was sure that he was lying and that he did know Handon Gar and that it was quite possible that the man might be in this very camp, but I saw that it was useless to pursue the question further as it would only make Tunzo Bor all the more suspicious of me.

We were worked very hard and were underfed. It seemed to me that the Kapars were very stupid; they need labor, yet they treat the men in labor camps so badly that the mortality rate is much higher than necessary. I noticed that the Kapars are always pressed for food, but they are extremely shortsighted to beat men to death for nothing or overwork them so they drop in their tracks, when these same men might be producing more food for them.

The lot of the free workers is a little better, but not much; they are serfs, but they are not locked up in prison camps. However, they are overworked and treated cruelly, although many of them are native Kapars as well as peoples of conquered countries. The soldiers fare much better than the workers, and the members of the Zabo live well, for everyone is afraid of them; even the army officers and those highly placed politically live little better, though they live off the fat of the land, if there is any fat in Kapara.

After a week of hard labor and poor food, I was given an easy job, working in the garden of the officer in charge of the camp. An armed guard always accompanied me and remained with me while I worked. He did not abuse me, nor did any of the guards in the prison compound. I was even given good food occasionally from the officer's kitchen. I could not understand it, but I was afraid to ask any questions, but finally the guard himself volunteered some information.

"Who are you, anyway?" he demanded.

"I am No. 267M9436," I replied.

"No," he said; "I mean what is your name?"

"I thought we weren't supposed to use any names," I reminded him.

"If I tell you to, you can," he said.

"Well, my name is Korvan Don," I replied.

"Where are you from?"

"Orvis."

He shook his head. "I can't understand it," he said.

"Understand what?" I asked.

"Why orders have been given that you shall be treated

so much better than the other prisoners," he explained; "and they come straight from Gurrul, too."

"I'm sure I don't know," I replied, but I had an idea that it might be because Gurrul was still investigating me and might be coming to the conclusion that I could be of value to the Kapars. I knew perfectly well that I wasn't being treated this way because of any humanitarian reasons.

CHAPTER FOUR

WHEN THE SKY is not overcast, the Polodian nights are gorgeous in the extreme. There is a constant procession of planets passing across the heavens, following each other in stately procession throughout the night; and thus clear nights are quite well lighted, especially by the nearer planets.

It was on such a clear night, about three weeks after I had been brought to the prison camp, that a fellow prisoner came close to me and whispered, "I am Handon Gar."

I scrutinized him very closely to see if I could recognize him from the description given me by the Commissioner for War.

This man was terribly emaciated and looked like an old man, but gradually I recognized him. He must have been subjected to the cruelest of treatment during the two years that he had been here.

"Yes," I said presently, "I recognize you."

"How can you recognize me?" he demanded, instantly suspicious; "I do not know you, and you never knew me, but Tunzo Bor told me you were inquiring about me. Who are you, and what do you want?"

"I recognized you from the description given me by the Commissioner for War," I explained. "I know that you are Handon Gar, and that I can trust you. My name is Tangor; I am known here as Korvan Don. I was sent here on a mission by the Eljanhai and the Commissioner for War,"

I continued in a low whisper, "and was instructed to ascertain what your fate had been."

He smiled sourly. "And now you are in the same boat as I; I'm afraid they'll never learn what became of either of us."

"Is Tunzo Bor all right?" I asked.

"Yes, but he suspected you. However, I did too, but I couldn't see how I could be any worse off if I told you my name. I do not recall ever having heard yours. Where did you live in Unis, and what did you do?"

"I lived in Orvis and was a pilot in the fighting service."

"It is strange that I never met you," he said, and I could see that he was becoming suspicious again.

"It is not so strange," I said; "I am sure that I know only a very few of the thousands of pilots in the service; one could not know them all. Do you know Harkas Don?"

"Yes, indeed, very well," he replied.

"He is my best friend," I said.

He was silent for some time, and then he said, "How are Don's brothers?"

"He hasn't any," I replied; "they have all been killed in the war."

"And his sisters?" he asked.

"He only has one sister," I replied; "Yamoda. I saw her the night before I left. She had had an accident, but she is all right now."

"Well," he said, "if you know these people so intimately, you must be all right. You know we have to be careful here."

"Yes, I understand," I replied.

Again he was silent for a few moments, and then he leaned closer to me and whispered, "We are going to make a break in a few days; Tunzo Bor and I and a couple of others. We have it all planned. Do you want to come along?"

"I can't," I replied; "I haven't fulfilled my mission yet."

"You can't fulfill it while you're in a work camp," he said, "and you'll never get out. You might just as well make a break with us. If we get back to Orvis, I'll explain to the Eljanhai that I advised you to escape while there was a chance."

"No, thanks," I replied, "I shall get out of here."

"You seem very sure," he said, and I noticed that he looked at me peculiarly, and I had a feeling that he already regretted telling me what he had. I was about to try to reassure him, when a guard ordered us to stop talking.

A couple of days later, which was a rest day, a guard called to me to come over to the wire fence, and there I found Morga Sagra awaiting me. It was quite unusual for prisoners to be allowed to have visitors, and I could see that it aroused a great deal of interest and comment in the compound.

"I have been working hard for your release," she told me in a whisper, "but Gurrul is still unconvinced. If you have heard of anything suspicious here—anything the Zabo would like to know—if you will report it, it will prove that you are all right, and it will be much easier to get you out."

"I have heard nothing," I said; "we are not allowed to do much talking, and anyway, everyone here is suspicious of everyone else."

"Well, keep your ears open, though I think that I'll soon have you out anyway. The thing that has Gurrul guessing is your appearance; you know, you don't look much like a native of any Polodian country; and so he is commencing to think that your story of your origin may be true."

"How are you getting along?" I asked her.

"All right," she said. "I have a nice apartment, and they are treating me all right, but I am always being watched; however, it is a grand place to live; these are real people; they live for war—a great race, a noble race."

"And a very hospitable people," I said.

Her eyes narrowed. "Be careful, Korvan Don," she said. "You can go too far even with me. Remember that I am a Kapar now."

I laughed. "You always insist on putting the wrong interpretation on things I say, Sagra."

"I hope so," she snapped.

Shortly after she left, Handon Gar approached me. "You'll get out all right, you damn cur," he whispered under his breath. "I know that woman, I always thought that she was a traitor. I suppose that you told her all about the plan Tunzo Bor and I have to escape."

Once again a guard interrupted and made us stop talking before I could explain. But could I explain? I was sorry that he believed as he did; but there was nothing that I could do about it, for I could not tell even him all the details of my mission.

And then, the very next day, his suspicions must have been definitely confirmed, as a messenger came from Gurrul with an order for my immediate release; and to make it appear all the worse, Morga Sagra accompanied the messenger and threw her arms around me.

I was taken by underground railway to Ergos and immediately to Gurrul's office in the headquarters building of the Zabo. He talked to me for about half an hour, asking me many questions concerning the other world and solar system from which I said I came.

"You certainly are no Polodian," he said; "there never was a human being like you, but I don't see how you could have been transported from another solar system."

"Neither do I," I admitted, "but there are many things in the universe that none of us understand."

"Well, Morga Sagra has vouched for you, and I am taking her word for it," he said; then he told me that quarters had been reserved for me, and that he would send a man with me to show me where they were located. "I think I can use you later on," he said; "so hold yourself in readiness. Do not leave your quarters without leaving word where you are going and never leave the city without my permission"; then he called into the room the man who was to show me to my quarters and dismissed me.

I knew that he was still suspicious of me, but that was not at all surprising as the secret police are always suspicious of everybody and everything. However, when I whispered to him some of the military secrets I had been ordered by the Eljanhai to give him orally, his attitude changed a little; and he was almost amiable as he bid me good-bye.

When I reached my new quarters, the door was opened by a rather nice-looking chap in the livery of a servant.

"This is your master, Korvan Don," said the green-uniformed Zabo agent who accompanied me.

The man bowed. "My name is Lotar Canl, sir," he said; "I hope that I shall be able to satisfy you."

Morga Sagra's apartment was in the same building as mine; and almost immediately we commenced to be invited out and entertained, but I had the feeling that we were being constantly watched. Well, so is everyone in Kapara. The entire nation lives in an atmosphere of intrigue and suspicion. The army fears the Zabo, the Zabo hates the army; everyone fears the five top men of the regime, each of whom fears the others. The head of the nation is called the Pom Da, literally the Great I. The present Pom Da has ruled for ten years. I suppose he had a name once, but it is never used; he is just the Great I, a cruel and cunning monster who has ordered many of his best friends and closest relatives destroyed.

Morga Sagra is a most sagacious girl; she was cut out by nature for intrigue, treason, and espionage. She thinks far ahead and lays her plans accordingly.

Everywhere that she went, she told people that I was from another world. She did this not so much to attract attention to me, but to help convince the Kapars that I had no ties in Unis and no reason to be loyal to that country. She wanted them to understand that I would be no traitor to Kapara, and eventually her plan bore fruit—the Great I sent for me.

Lotar Canl, my man, was evidently greatly impressed when he gave me the message. "You can go very far in Kapara, sir," he said, "if the Pom Da becomes interested in you; I am very proud to serve you, sir."

I already knew that I might go far if the Pom Da noticed me, but in what direction I was not certain—the paths of glory sometimes lead but to the grave.

CHAPTER FIVE

WHEN I REACHED the ornate building which houses the head of Kapara, I was first carefully searched for concealed weapons and then escorted by two heavily armed guards to a room presided over by a grim, elaborately uniformed and decorated official. Here I waited for about half an hour, my two guards sticking close to me; then the door at the far end of the room opened, and another officer appeared and called my name.

The guards arose with me and escorted me to the door of an enormous chamber, at the far end of which a man sat behind a huge desk. The guards were dismissed at the doorway and told to wait, and two officers took their places and escorted me the length of the room into the presence of the Pom Da.

He is not a large man, and I think that he appears even smaller than he is because of his very evident nervousness, fear, and suspicion.

He just sat and eyed me for what must have been a full minute before he spoke. His expression was venomous, seeming to reflect the deepest hatred; but I was to learn later that this expression was not reserved for anyone in particular; it was almost habitual with him, and this is understandable because his whole ideology is based on hate.

"So you are Korvan Don, the traitor?" he shot at me.

"I am no traitor," I said.

One of the officers seized me roughly by the arm. "When

you address the Pom Da," he shouted angrily, "always refer to him as the Highest Most High."

"You are betraying Unis," said the Pom Da, ignoring the interruption.

"Unis is not my country—Highest Most High."

"You claim to be from another world—from another solar system. Is that right?"

"Yes, Highest Most High," I replied.

"One Highest Most High in a conversation is sufficient," snapped the officer on my other side. I was learning Kaparan high etiquette the hard way.

The Pom Da questioned me for some time about the Earth and our solar system and how I could know how far away it was from Poloda. I explained everything to him to the best of my ability, but I doubt very much that he understood a great deal of what I said; the Kapars are not highly intelligent, their first Pom Da having killed off a majority of the intelligent people of his time and his successor destroying the remainder, leaving only scum to breed.

"What were you in that strange world from which you say you came?" he asked.

"I was a flier in the fighting forces of my country and also something of an inventor, having been at work on a ship in which I purposed traveling to another planet of our solar system."

"How far from your Earth would this planet be?" he asked.

"About 48,000,000 miles," I replied.

"That is a long way," he said. "Do you think that you could have done it?"

"I had high hopes; in fact, I was almost on the verge of perfecting my ship when I was called away to war."

"Tonos is less than six hundred thousand miles from Poloda," he mused. I could see that he had something on his mind, and I guessed what it was—or at least I hoped.

He talked to me for over a half an hour and then he dismissed me, but before I left I asked him if he would order my gold and jewels returned to me.

He turned to an officer standing at one end of his desk and instructed him to see that all of my belongings were returned to me; then the two officers and I backed out of the room. I had stood all during the interview, but that was not at all surprising as there was only one chair in the room and that was occupied by the Pom Da.

The green Zabo car took me back to my quarters, and the men who accompanied me were most obsequious; and when Lotar Canl opened the door and saw them bowing to me and calling me Most High, he beamed all over.

Morga Sagra came in from her apartment presently; and she was delighted with the honor that had been done me, and she didn't let any grass grow under her feet before she let it be known that I had been received by the Pom Da in an interview that lasted over a half an hour.

Now we commenced to be invited into the homes of the highest; and when my gold and jewels were returned, as they were the day after my interview with the Pom Da, Sagra and I were able to splurge a little bit; so that we had a gay time in the capital of Kapara, where only the very highest have a gay time, or even enough to eat.

Among our acquaintances was a woman named Gimmel Gora, with whom Morga Sagra had associated while I was in the prison camp; and she and her man, Grunge, were with us a great deal. They were not married, but then no one in Kapara is married; such silly, sentimental things as marriages were done away with nearly a hundred years ago. I did not like either Gimmel Gora or Grunge; in fact, I did not like any of the Kapars I had met so far, with the possible exception of my man, Lotar Canl; and, of course, I even suspected him of being an agent of the Zabo.

The Kapars are arrogant, supercilious, stupid, and rude; and Grunge was no exception. I did not know what he did for a living; and, of course, I never asked, as I never showed the slightest curiosity about anything. If a stranger asks too many questions in Kapara, he is quite likely to find his head rolling around on the floor—they don't waste ammunition in Kapara.

We were making a lot of acquaintances, but I was not getting anyplace with my mission. I was no nearer learning about the amplifier than I had been in Orvis. I kept talking about the ship I had been inventing in my own world, hoping in that way to get a hint from someone that would lead me on the right trail; but after two months in Ergos, I hadn't been able to get the slightest lead; it was just as though no such thing as a new powerful amplifier existed, and I commenced to wonder if the Commissioner for War had been misinformed.

One day a green car stopped before the building in which my apartment was located. Lotar Canl, who had been at a front window, saw it, and when a summons came at our door, he looked at me apprehensively. "I hope that you have not been indiscreet," he said as he went to open the door.

I, too, hoped that I hadn't; for these grim, green-uniformed men do not call on one for the purpose of playing rummy or hopscotch.

"Korvan Don?" asked one of the men, looking at me.

I nodded, "Yes."

"Come with us."

That was all—just like that: "Come with us."; just, "Come with us."

I came, and they whisked me away to that horrible building with the carved facade, where I was ushered into Gurrul's office.

He gave me that venomous stare of his for about a half a minute before he spoke. "Do you know what happens to people who have knowledge of crimes against the state and do not report them to the authorities?" he demanded.

"I think I can guess," I replied.

"Well, four men have escaped from the prison camp in which you were confined."

"I do not see how that concerns me," I said.

He had a large file of papers on the desk before him, and he thumbed through them. "Here," he said, "I find that on several dates you were found talking to Handon Gar and Tunzo Bor—in whispers!"

"That is the only way one may talk there," I replied.

He thumbed through the papers again. "It seems that you were extremely familiar with Tunzo Bor from the time you entered camp; you were evidently very familiar with both of these men, although I find no record that you were particularly familiar with the other two who escaped. Now," he shouted, "what were you whispering about?"

"I was questioning them," I said.

"Why?" he demanded.

"I question whomever I can for such information as I may get. You see, I was in the Zabo in my own country; so it is natural for me to acquire all the information I can from the enemy."

"Did you get any information?"

"I think I was about to when Morga Sagra came to see me; after that they wouldn't talk to me."

"Before Handon Gar escaped he told several prisoners that you were a spy from Unis."

As he growled this out, Gurrul looked as though he would like to chop my head off himself.

I laughed. "I told him that myself," I said. "He evidently wanted to get even with me for almost fooling him."

Gurrul nodded. "An intelligent agent would have done that very thing," he said. "I am glad that you have been able to clear yourself, as this is the first bad report I have had concerning you"; then he dismissed me.

As I walked slowly toward my apartment, just about a half a mile from the Zabo headquarters, I reviewed in my mind my interview with Gurrul; and I came to realize that he had exonerated me altogether too willingly. It was not like him. I had a feeling that he was still suspicious of me, and that he had done this to throw me off my guard that I might be more easily trapped if I were indeed disloyal. This conviction was definitely heightened before I reached my apartment. I had occasion to stop in two shops on the way; and, on each occasion, when I left the shop I saw the same man loitering nearby; I was being shadowed, and in a very crude and amateurish way at that. I thought that if the Zabo were no more efficient in other respects, I would have little to fear from them; but I did not let this belief lessen my caution.

Before I reached my apartment, I met Grunge, who was walking with a man I did not know, and whom he introduced as Horthal Wend. Horthal was a middle-aged man with a very kindly face, which certainly differentiated him from most of the other Kapars I had met.

They invited me into a drinking place and because I believed Grunge to be connected in some way with the Zabo, I accepted. Grunge had no visible means of support, yet he was always well supplied with money; and, for that reason, I suspected him of being either a member or a tool of the secret police. I felt that if I associated with men of this stamp and was always careful of what I said and did, only good reports of me could reach Gurrul. I also made it a point to try to never be alone with anyone—and never to whisper; there is nothing that makes a member of the Zabo more suspicious than a whisper.

Grunge and Horthal Wend ordered wine. Grunge had to show a wine card in order to obtain it; and this strengthened my belief that he was connected with the Zabo, for only those who stand well with the government are issued wine cards.

When I ordered a nonalcoholic drink, Grunge urged me to take wine; but I refused, as I never drink anything of the sort when I have an important duty to fulfill.

Grunge seemed quite put out to think that I would not drink wine with him, and that convinced me that he had hoped that wine would loosen my tongue—a very moldy trick of secret police. I found Horthal Wend as kindly in manner as in appearance, and I took quite a liking to him. Before I left him, he had extracted a promise from me that I would come and see him and his woman and bring Morga Sagra with me.

Little did I dream then what the death of this kindly man would mean to me.

CHAPTER SIX

THE FOLLOWING EVENING, Sagra and I had dinner with Grunge and Gimmel Gora; and during the course of the evening, I mentioned Horthal Wend and remarked that I had found him most intelligent and friendly.

"I guess that he is intelligent enough," said Grunge, "but I find him a little too pleasant; that, to me, is an indication of sentimentality and softness, neither of which have any place in Kapar manhood. However, he stands very well with the Pom Da, and is, therefore, a safe man to know and cultivate, for our beloved Pom Da is never wrong in his estimate of men—in fact, he is never wrong in anything."

I could not help but think that if sentiment and intelligence had no place in Kapar manhood, Grunge was an ideal Kapar.

Grunge's use of the word beloved might seem to belie my statement that he was without sentiment, but it was really only the fawning expression of a sycophant and connoted more of fear than love.

I was constantly mentally comparing Kapars with the Unisans. Here in Kapara all is suspicion and fear—fear of unseen malign forces that are all powerful; fear of your next-door neighbor; fear of your servants; fear of your best friend, and suspicion of all.

All during the evening, Sagra had seemed distrait. Grunge, on the contrary, was quite talkative and almost affable. He directed most of his conversation and elephantine wit at

Sagra and was correspondingly disagreeable and sarcastic when he spoke to Gimmel Gora.

He was meticulously polite to me, which was unusual; as Grunge was seldom if ever polite to anyone of whom he was not afraid. "We have much to be thankful for in the wonderful friendship that has developed between us," he said to me; "it seems as though I had known you always, Korvan Don. It is not often in this life that two men meet who may mutually trust each other on short acquaintance."

"You are quite right," I said, "but I think one learns to know almost instinctively who may be trusted and who may not." I wondered what he was driving at, and I did not have to wait long to discover.

"You have been in Kapara for some time, now," he continued, "and I suppose that some of your experiences could not have been entirely pleasant; for instance the prison camp and the prison beneath the Zabo headquarters."

"Well, of course, freedom is always to be preferred to confinement," I replied; "but I have sense enough to realize that every precaution must be taken in a nation at war, and I admire the Kapars for their efficiency in this respect. While I did not enjoy being confined, I have no complaint to make, as I was well treated." If one may instinctively recognize a trustworthy friend, one may also instinctively recognize an unscrupulous enemy; and this I felt Grunge to be, for I was confident that he was attempting to cajole me into making some criticism that would incriminate me in the eyes of the Zabo.

He looked a little crestfallen, but he said, "I am glad to hear you say that. Just between friends, tell me in confidence what you thought of Gurrul."

"A highly intelligent man, well fitted for the post he occupies," I replied. "Although he must have to contend with all types of criminals, scoundrels, and traitors, he appears to me to be fair and just, without being soft or

"Here in Kapara all is suspicion and fear."

sentimental." I was learning to talk like a Kapar and to lie like one too.

As Sagra and I walked home that night, I asked her what had been troubling her, for she had not seemed herself at all.

"I am worried and frightened," she replied; "Grunge has been making advances to me, and Gimmel Gora knows it. I am afraid of both of them, for I believe that both are agents of the Zabo."

"Neither one of us has anything to fear," I said. "Aren't we both good Kapars?"

"I sometimes wonder if you are," she said.

"At first I may have been a little critical," I said, "but that was before I understood the strength and beauty of their system. Now I am as good a Kapar as there is." From this speech it might be assumed that I was suspicious of Morga Sagra, and the assumption would be wholly correct. I was suspicious of Morga Sagra, of Grunge, of Gimmel Gora, of Lotar Canl, my man—in fact, of everybody. In this respect, at least, I had become a good Kapar.

When I got home that night, I found that my quarters had been thoroughly ransacked. The contents of every drawer was scattered about on the floor; my rugs had been torn up, and my mattress cut open.

While I was viewing the havoc, Lotar Canl came home. He looked around the place, and then, with the faintest of smiles on his lips he said, "Burglars. I hope that they got nothing of value, sir."

Most of my gold and jewels are deposited in a safe place; but in addition to that which I carry on my person, I had left a handful of gold in one of the drawers in my desk, and this I found scattered on the floor—all of it.

"Well," I said, "they overlooked this gold, and there was nothing else in the apartment anybody would wish."

"They must have been frightened away before they could gather this up," said Lotar Canl.

The little game that he and I were playing was almost

laughable for neither of us dared suggest the truth—that the apartment had been searched by the police.

"I am glad," he said, "that you had nothing of value here other than this gold."

When I met Sagra the next day, I said nothing about the matter to her, for I had learned that no matter how often one's home is "burglarized" or even if his grandmother is taken at midnight and beheaded, he does not mention the occurrence to anyone; but Sagra was less reticent. She told me that she was being constantly watched; that her room had been searched three times, and that she was terrified. "I have a secret enemy," she said, "who is leaving no stone unturned to get me destroyed."

"Have you any idea who it is?" I asked.

"Yes," she said, "I think I know."

"Gimmel Gora?"

She nodded, and then she whispered, "And you must be careful of Grunge. He thinks that you are my man, and he would like to get rid of you."

There had never been any suggestion of any sentimental relationship between Morga Sagra and me. She had used me in order to get to Kapara; and because we had been two strangers in a strange land, we had been constantly thrown together since. I know that she enjoyed my company, and I still found her witty and entertaining when she was not entirely preoccupied with the terror which now obsessed her. If ever a just retribution were being meted to a person, this was the instance. I was confident that Morga Sagra would have given her soul to have been back in Unis; and to her terror was added hopelessness, for she knew that she could never return.

That evening we went to call on Horthal Wend and his woman, Haka Gera. She was a heavy-minded, rather stupid woman, but evidently a good housekeeper and probably a good manager, which I judged Horthal Wend needed, for he was evidently easygoing and careless.

We talked about art, literature, music, the weather, and the wonders of Kapar ideology—about the only safe subject for discussion in Kapara; and even then we had to be careful. If one should by mistake express appreciation of some work of art or musical composition by a person in bad odor with the heads of the state or with the Zabo, that was treason.

During the evening, their fourteen-year-old son, Horthal Gyl, joined us. He was a precocious child, and I do not like precocious children. He was a loud-mouthed little egotist who knew it all, and he kept projecting himself into the conversation until he practically monopolized it.

Horthal Wend was evidently very proud of him and very fond of him; but once when he made a gesture as though to caress the lad, the boy struck his hand away.

"None of that!" he growled at his father; "such maudlin sentimentality is not for Kapar men. I am ashamed of you."

"Now, now," said his mother gently; "it is not wrong for your father to love you."

"I do not wish him to love me," snapped the boy. "I only wish that he should admire me and be proud of me because I am hard. I do not want him or anyone to be as ashamed of me as I am of him because of his sentimentality and softness."

Horthal Wend tried to smile as he shook his head. "You see, he is a good Kapar," he said; and, I thought, a little sadly.

"I see," I said.

The boy shot me a quick suspicious look. Evidently I had not kept my innermost feelings out of those two words.

We left shortly after this and as we walked home, I was conscious of a feeling of great depression. I think it was caused by the attitude of that son to his father. "Horthal Gyl will grow up to be a fine example of the Kapar gentlemen," I said.

"I would rather not discuss him," replied Sagra.

CHAPTER SEVEN

I WENT TO BED immediately after reaching my apartment. Lotar Canl had asked for the entire night off; so when I was awakened shortly after midnight by a summons at my door, I had to answer it myself. As I opened it, two green-clad Zabo troopers stepped in with drawn pistols.

"Dress and come with us," said one of them.

"There must be some mistake," I said; "I am Korvan Don, you can't want me."

"Shut up and get dressed," said the one who had first spoken, "or we'll take you along in your nightclothes."

While I was dressing, I racked my brains trying to think what I had done to deserve arrest. Of course I knew it would be useless to ask these men. Even if they knew, which they probably did not, they wouldn't tell me. Naturally I thought of Grunge, because of what Morga Sagra had told me, but the man could not possibly have had anything to report against me; although, of course, he could have fabricated some story.

I was taken directly to Gurrul's office; and although it was well after midnight, he was still there. He gave me one of his most terrible looks and then screamed at me, "So you slipped at last, you filthy spy. I have always suspected you, and I am always right."

"I don't know what you are talking about," I said. "You can have absolutely no charge against me; because I have spoken no treasonable words since I came to Kapara.

I defy anyone to prove that I am not as good a Kapar as you."

"Oh," he barked, "so you haven't said anything treasonable? Well, you idiot, you have written it"; and he took a small red book from a drawer in his desk and held it up in front of me and shook it in my face. "Your diary, you fool." He turned the leaves and scanned the pages for a moment and then he read, "'Gurrul is a fat idiot'; so I am a fat idiot, am I?" He turned a few more pages, and read again. "'The Zabo is made up of moronic murderers; and when our revolution succeeds, I shall have them all beheaded. I shall behead Gurrul myself.' What do you say to that?"

"I say that I never saw that book before and that I never wrote any of the things which you have read."

He turned over some more pages and read again, "'The Pom Da is an egotistical maniac and will be one of the first to be destroyed when J and I rule Kapara.' Who is J?", he bellowed at me.

"I haven't the slightest idea," I told him.

"Well, there are ways of making you find out," he said, and getting up and coming around the end of his desk, he knocked me down before I had the slightest idea what his intentions were.

I leaped to my feet with the intention of handing him what he had handed me, but several troopers seized me. "Secure his hands," ordered Gurrul, and they put them behind my back and snapped handcuffs about my wrists.

"You'd better tell me who J is," said Gurrul, "or you'll get a great deal worse than what I just gave you. Who is this accomplice of yours? It will go easier with you if you tell me."

"I do not know who J is," I said.

"Take him into the question box," ordered Gurrul, and they took me into an adjoining room which I instantly saw was fitted up as a torture chamber. They let me look around the room for a moment at the various instruments of torture, and then Gurrul started demanding again that I tell him who J was. He kept striking me repeatedly, and when I fell he kicked me.

When I still insisted that I didn't know, one of them burned me with a hot iron.

"Your right eye goes next," said Gurrul; "who is J?"

They worked on me for about an hour, and I was pretty nearly dead when they finally gave up.

"Well," said Gurrul, "I can't spend all the rest of the night with this stubborn fool; take him downstairs and behead him—unless in the meantime he tells you who J is."

Well, this was the end of my mission. I had learned absolutely nothing, and now I was to be beheaded. As a spy I was evidently a total failure. A couple of them jerked me roughly to my feet; for I could not rise by myself, and just then the door opened and Lotar Canl entered the room. When I saw him, my suspicions were confirmed, as I had always thought that he was probably a Zabo agent; and now I thought that it was probably he who had turned this forged diary over to them, probably in the hope of winning preferment by discovering this plot against the nation.

He took in the scene in a quick glance and then he turned to Gurrul. "Why is this man here?"

"He is a traitor who was conspiring against Kapara," replied Gurrul. "We found the evidence of his guilt in this diary in his desk."

"I thought as much," said Lotar Canl, "when I came home earlier than I expected tonight and found that the book had been removed from his desk."

"You knew about this book," demanded Gurrul.

"Of course," replied Lotar Canl. "I saw it planted there. Korvan Don knew nothing about it. I have watched this man most carefully since he has been here. He is as good a Kapar as any of us."

Gurrul looked a little sheepish, that is if a wolf can look sheepish. "Who put the book in his desk?" he asked.

"The man who actually placed it there was an innocent tool," replied Lotar Canl. "I have him under arrest. He is in the next room under guard. I wish that you would question him yourself."

The man was brought in, and Gurrul showed him the diary and asked him if he had placed it in my desk.

The poor fellow was trembling so that he could scarcely speak, but finally he managed to say, "Yes, Most High."

"Why did you do it?" demanded Gurrul.

"The night before last, a man came into my room shortly after midnight. He flashed a tiny light on a Zabo badge he wore, but he was careful not to shine it on his face. He told me that I had been selected to place this book in Korvan Don's desk. He said that it was a command from you, Most High."

Gurrul called Lotal Canl to the far end of the room, and they whispered together for several minutes; then Gurrul came back. "You may go," he said to the man, "but understand that nobody ever came to your room in the middle of the night and asked you to put anything in anybody's desk; you were not brought here tonight; you did not see me nor anyone else who is in this room. Do you understand?"

"Yes, Most High," replied the man.

"Take him away and see that he is returned to his home," Gurrul directed the two agents who had brought the fellow in; then he turned again to me. "Mistakes are bound to occur occasionally," he said. "It is regrettable, but it is so. Have you any idea who might have had that book placed in your desk?"

I thought that it was Grunge, but I said, "I haven't any idea; as far as I know I haven't an enemy in Kapara. There is no reason why anyone should wish to get me into trouble." I suspected that Grunge was a Zabo agent, and I knew that if he were I would probably get myself into trouble by accusing him. Gurrul turned to one of his officers. "Have this man taken to a hospital," he said, "and see that he receives the best of treatment"; and then he turned to me. "You are never to mention this unfortunate occurrence to anyone. While returning home, you were knocked down and run over. Do you understand?"

I told him that I did; and then they sent for a stretcher, and I was carried out and taken to a hospital.

The next day, Sagra came to see me. She said that she had found a note under her door telling her that I had been in an accident and what hospital I was in.

"Yes," I said, "I was hit by an automobile."

She looked frightened. "Do you think that you will be hit again?" she asked.

"I hope not by the same automobile," I said.

"I am terribly frightened," she said; "I am afraid that it will be my turn next."

"Keep out of the way of automobiles," I advised her.

"Gimmel Gora won't speak to me anymore, and Grunge won't leave me alone. He told me not to be afraid, as he is a Zabo agent."

"Just as I thought," I said, "and a hit-and-run driver too."

"I wish I were back in Orvis," she said.

"Be careful what you say, Sagra," I advised.

She looked at me with wide, frightened eyes. "You, too?" she asked.

"No, not I," I assured her; "but the walls may have ears."

"I wish you could tell me what happened," she said.

I shook my head. "I have told you—I was hit by an automobile and run over."

"I suppose you are right," she said; "and I also suppose that I have talked altogether too much; but I am nearly crazy, and if I didn't have someone to tell my fears to, I think I should go crazy."

Treason is a terrible thing, and its punishment must be terrible.

CHAPTER EIGHT

I WAS IN THE HOSPITAL for about two weeks; but at last I was discharged and allowed to go home, although I had to remain in bed there most of the time. I found a new man there to take Lotar Canl's place. He had brought a note from Lotar Canl saying that he knew that I would need someone as soon as I returned from the hospital and that he could highly recommend this man, whose name was Danul.

Lotar Canl came to see me himself the day after I was returned from the hospital. While we were talking, he wrote something on a piece of paper and handed it to me. It read, "Danul is not connected with the Zabo, but he is a good Kapar"; then, after I had read it, he took the paper from me and burned it up; but he was very careful to see that Danul was not around to observe what he did.

It is terrible to live under this constant strain of fear and suspicion, and it shows in the faces of most of these people. Lotar Canl was peculiarly free from it, and I always enjoyed talking with him; however, we were both careful never to touch on any forbidden subjects.

While I was in Ergos, there was scarcely a day passed that I did not hear the detonation of Unisan bombs; and I could visualize my comrades in arms flying high over this buried city. The only reports that I ever heard of these activities always related Kapar victories; or the great number of enemy planes shot down, and the very small losses suffered by the Kapars, or they would tell of the terrific bombing of Orvis or of other Unisan cities. According to these official reports, Kapara was just on the verge of winning the war.

Harkas Yamoda was much in my mind at this time, and thoughts of her and my other friends in Orvis rather depressed me, because I felt that I couldn't return until I had fulfilled my mission, and I seemed to be as far as ever from that. No matter how often I brought up the subject of my invention, no one ever indicated that he had heard of such a thing. It was very disheartening, as the first step to acquiring any information about the new amplifier was to learn who was working on it; and of course I didn't dare suggest in the slightest way that I had knowledge that any such thing was being considered in Kapara.

Sagra came to see me every day and spent a great deal of time with me, and one day Grunge came. "I was very sorry to hear of your accident," he said; "and I intended to come and see you sooner, but I have been very busy. There are many careless drivers in Ergos; one cannot be too careful."

"Oh, well," I said, "perhaps it was my fault; I was probably careless in crossing the street."

"One cannot be too careful," he said again.

"I have found that out," I replied; "even a friend might run over one."

He gave me a quick look. He did not stay very long, and it was evident that he was nervous and ill at ease while he was there. I was glad when he left, for the more I saw of the man the less I liked him.

Horthal Wend and his woman and son came on another day while Sagra was there. Horthal Wend said that he had only just heard of my accident and was greatly distressed to think that he had not known of it before and come to see me earlier. He did not question me as to the cause of it, but Horthal Gyl did.

"I was hit by an automobile, knocked down and run over," I told him. He gave a knowing look and started to say something, but his father interrupted him. "Gyl has just made his mother and me very proud," he said; "he stood at the head of his class for the year," and he looked adoringly at the boy.

"What are you studying?" I asked, in order to be polite and not that I gave a continental hang what he was studying.

"What do you suppose a Kapar man studies?" he demanded impudently. "War."

"How interesting," I commented.

"But that is not all I study," he continued. "However, what else I study is the business only of my instructor and myself."

"And you expect to be a fighter when you grow up, I suppose," I said, for I saw that it pleased Horthal Wend that I should be taking an interest in his son.

"When I grow up, I'm going to be a Zabo agent," said the boy; "I am always practicing."

"How do you practice for that?" I asked.

"Don't show too much curiosity about the Zabo," he warned; "it is not healthful."

I laughed at him and told him that I was only politely interested in the subject.

"I have warned you," he said.

"Don't be impolite, son," Horthal Wend admonished him.

"If I were you," he retorted, "I wouldn't interfere with the Zabo; and you should be more careful with whom you associate," and he cast a dark look at Sagra. "The Zabo sees all; knows all." I should have liked to have choked the impossible little brat. Sagra looked uncomfortable and Horthal Wend fidgeted.

Finally he said, "Oh, stop talking about the Zabo, son; it's bad enough to have it without talking about it all the time."

The boy shot him a dirty look. "You are speaking treason," he said to his father.

"Now, Gyl," said his mother, "I wouldn't say things like that."

I could see that Horthal Wend was getting more and more nervous, and presently he got up and they took their leave.

"Somebody ought to give that brat rat poison," I said to Sagra.

She nodded. "He is dangerous," she whispered. "He hangs around Grunge's home a great deal and is very friendly with both Grunge and Gimmel Gora. I think it is through Gimmel Gora that he has come to suspect me; did you see how he looked at me when he told his father that he should be more careful with whom he associated?"

"Yes," I said, "I noticed; but I wouldn't worry about him, he is only a little boy practicing at being a detective."

"Nevertheless, he is a very dangerous little boy," she said. "A great deal of the information that the Zabo receives comes from children."

A couple of days later I went out for my first walk; and as Horthal Wend lived only a short distance from my apartment, I went over to call on him.

Haka Gera, his woman, opened the door for me. She was in tears, and the boy was sitting, sullen and scowling, in the corner. I sensed that something terrible had happened, but I was afraid to ask. At last, between sobs, Haka Gera said, "You came to see Wend?"

"Yes," I replied; "is he at home?"

She shook her head and then burst into a violent spasm of sobbing. The boy sat there and glowered at her. Finally she gained control of herself and whispered, "They came last night and took him away." She looked over at the boy, and there was fear in her eyes—fear and horror and reproach.

I did my best to comfort her; but it was hopeless, and

finally I took my departure. As far as I know, Horthal Wend was never seen nor heard of again.

I am not a drinking man; but as I walked back toward my apartment, I was so depressed and almost nauseated by the whole affair that I went into a drinking place and ordered a glass of wine. There were only two other customers in the place as I seated myself at a little table. They had the hard, cruel faces of Kapar fighting men or police. I could see that they were scrutinizing me closely and whispering to one another. Finally they got up and came over and stopped in front of me.

"Your credentials," barked one of them.

My wine permit was lying on the table in front of me, and I pushed it over toward him. It bore my name and address and a brief description. He picked it up and looked at it and then threw it down on the table angrily. "I said your credentials," he snapped.

"Let me see yours," I said; "I have the right to know upon what authority you question a law-abiding citizen." I was right in my demand, although possibly a little foolish in insisting upon my rights. The fellow grumbled and showed me a Zabo badge, and then I handed him my credentials.

He looked them over carefully and then handed them back. "So you're the fellow who was run over by an automobile a few weeks ago," he said; "well, if I were you, I'd be more respectful to Zabo officers, or you may be run over again"; and then they turned and stamped out of the place. It was such things as this that made life in Ergos what it was.

When I got home, Danul told me that two Zabo agents had been there and searched my apartment. I don't know why he told me; because he really had no business to, unless he had been given orders to do so for the purpose of trapping me into some treasonable expression, for it is treason to express any disapproval of an act of the Zabo;

I could have been drawn and quartered for what I was thinking of them, though.

Now I commenced to be suspicious of Danul, and I wondered if Lotar Canl had lied to me or if this man was an agent without Lotar Canl having any knowledge of the fact. Insofar as suspicion was concerned, I was becoming a true Kapar; I suspected everybody. I think the only man whom I had ever met here that I had perfect confidence in was Horthal Wend, and they had come at night and taken him away.

CHAPTER NINE

MORGA SAGRA came in shortly after I returned; and I sent Danul out on an errand, so that I might tell her about Horthal Wend.

"That horrible child!" she exclaimed. "Oh, Tangor!" she cried, "can't we get out of here?"

"Don't ever speak that name again," I said. "Do you want to get me into trouble?"

"I'm sorry; it just came out. Couldn't we get away somehow?"

"And be shot as soon as we return to Orvis?" I said. "You got yourself into this," I reminded her, "and now you've got to grin and bear it and so have I; although I really enjoy it here," I lied. "I wouldn't go back to Orvis under any circumstances."

She looked at me questioningly. "I'm sorry," she said. "You won't hold it against me, will you? Oh, Korvan Don, you won't tell anybody that I said that?"

"Of course not," I assured her.

"I can't help it," she said, "I can't help it. I am almost a nervous wreck. I have a premonition that something terrible is going to happen," and just then there came a pounding on the door, and I thought that Morga Sagra was going to faint.

"Pull yourself together and buck up," I said, as I crossed to the door.

As I opened it, I was confronted by two high officers of the Kapar fighting force.

"You are Korvan Don?" inquired one of them.

"I am," I replied.

"You will come with us," he said.

Well, at least they were not agents of the Zabo; but what they wanted of me I couldn't imagine; and, of course, I did not ask. Since I have been here in Ergos, I have schooled myself to such an extent that I even hesitate to ask the time of day. We were driven at high speed, through crowded streets, to the building in which is the office of the Pom Da, and, after but a moment's wait in an anteroom, I was ushered into the presence of the Great I.

The Pom Da came to the point immediately. "When you were here before," he said, "you told me that before you left that other world from which you say you came, you were working on a ship which you believed would have a radius of something like 48,000,000 miles. One of our foremost inventors has been working along similar lines, and had almost perfected a power amplifier which would make it possible for a ship to fly from Poloda to other planets of our solar system; but unfortunately he recently suffered an accident and died.

"Naturally this important work was carried on with the utmost secrecy. He had no assistants; nobody but he could complete the experimental amplifier upon which he was working. It must be completed.

"I have had excellent reports of your integrity and loyalty since you have been here. I have sent for you because I believe you are the man best fitted to carry on from where our late inventor left off. It is, naturally, a very important piece of work, the details of which must be guarded carefully lest they fall into the hands of our enemy, who treacherously maintains agents among us. I have convinced myself that you are to be trusted, and I am never wrong in my estimate of men. You will therefore proceed to the laboratory and workshop where the amplifier was being built and complete it."

"Is it a command, Highest Most High?" I asked.

"It is," he replied.

"Then I shall do my best," I said, "but it is a responsibility I should not have chosen voluntarily, and I cannot have but wished that you might have found someone better fitted than I for so important a commission." I wished to give him the impression that I was reluctant to work upon the amplifier, for fear that I might otherwise reveal my elation. After weeks of failure and disappointment, and without the faintest ray of hope of ever succeeding in my mission, the solution of my problem was now being dumped into my lap by the highest Kapar in the land.

The Great I, who was such a marvelous judge of men, gave me a few general instructions and then ordered that I be taken at once to the laboratory; and I backed out of his presence with the two officers who had brought me. I thought that I understood now, why I had been watched so closely, and why my apartment had been ransacked so frequently.

As I drove through the streets of Ergos, I was happy for the first time since I had left Orvis; and I was rather pleased with myself too, for I felt confident that my oft-repeated references to the imaginary ship that I had been supposed to have been working on on Earth had finally borne fruit. Of course, I had never been working on any such ship as I described; but I had done considerable experimental work on airplane motors, and I hoped that this would help me in my present undertaking.

I was driven to a neighborhood with which I was very familiar and was taken to a laboratory behind a home in which I had been entertained—the home of Horthal Wend.

I spent a full week studying the plans and examining the small model, and the experimental amplifier that was

"I spent a full week studying the plans and examining the small model."

almost completed. Horthal Wend had kept voluminous notes, and from these I discovered that he had eliminated all the bugs but one. As I worked, I was occasionally aware of being watched; and a couple of times I caught a fleeting glimpse of a face at the window. But whether the Pom Da was having me watched or someone was awaiting an opportunity to steal the plans, I did not know.

The trouble with Horthal Wend's amplifier was that it diffused instead of concentrating the energy derived from the sun, so that, while I was confident that it would propel a ship to either of the nearer planets, the speed would diminish progressively as the distance from the central power station on Poloda increased, with the result that the time consumed in covering the six hundred thousand miles between the two planets would be so great as to render the invention useless from any practical standpoint.

On the day that I eliminated the last bug and felt sure that I had an amplifier capable of powering the ship to almost any distance from Poloda, I caught a glimpse of that face at the window again, and decided to try to find out who it was who was so inquisitive about my work.

Pretending that I had noticed nothing, I busied myself about the room, keeping my back toward the window as much as possible, until I finally reached the door that was near the window; then I threw the door open and stepped out. There was Horthal Gyl, very red in the face and looking very foolish.

"What are you doing here?" I demanded; "practicing again, or trying to pry into government secrets?"

Horthal Gyl got hold of himself in a hurry; the brat had the brazen effrontery of a skunk on a narrow trail. "What I am doing here is none of your business," he said impudently. "There may be those who trust you, but I don't."

"Whether you trust me or not, is of no interest to me," I said, "but if I ever catch you here again, I am going to give you all of the beatings in one that your father should have given you." He gave me one of his foul looks and turned and walked away.

The next day I asked for an interview with the Pom Da, who granted it immediately. The officers who came for me and those whom I encountered on my way to the office of the Great I were most obsequious; I was getting places in Kapara in a big way. Any man who could ask for an audience with the Pom Da and get it immediately was a man to kowtow to.

"How is the work progressing?" he asked me as I stopped before his desk.

"Excellently," I replied. "I am sure that I can perfect the amplifier if you will place a plane at my disposal for experimental purposes."

"Certainly," he said. "What type of plane do you wish?"

"The fastest scout plane you have," I replied.

"Why do you want a fast plane," he demanded, instantly suspicious.

"Because it is the type of plane that will have to be used for the first experimental flight to another planet," I replied.

He nodded and beckoned to one of his aides. "Have a fast scout plane placed at Korvan Don's disposal," he ordered, "and issue instructions that he is to be permitted to fly at any time at his discretion." I was so elated that I could have hugged even the Pom Da; and then he added, "but give orders that a flying officer must always accompany him." My bubble was burst.

I made several experimental flights; and I always took along all the plans, drawings, and the model. I took them quite openly, and I kept referring to Horthal Wend's notes, to the drawings, and to the model during the flight, giving the impression that I had to have them all with me in order to check the performance of the amplifier on the ship, as well as to prevent theft of them while I was away from the laboratory.

The same officer never accompanied me twice, a fact

which eventually had considerable bearing upon the performance of my mission. If these fellows could have known what was in my mind all the time they were sitting in the ship beside me, they would have been surprised; I was trying to think of some way in which I could kill them, for only by getting rid of them could I escape from Kapara.

The amplifier was an unqualified success; I was positive that it would fly the ship to any part of the solar system, but I didn't tell anybody so. I still insisted that a few experimental changes would have to be made, and so the time dragged on while I awaited an opportunity to kill the officer who accompanied me. The fact that they had never given me any weapons made this difficult.

I had not dared to ask for weapons; one does not go at anything of that kind directly, but I had tried to suggest that I should be armed by telling the Pom Da that I had seen someone looking in my laboratory window on several occasions. All that got me was a heavy guard of Zabo agents around the laboratory building.

Since I had been working on the amplifier, I had seen practically nothing of Morga Sagra, as I had slept in the laboratory and had only returned to my apartment occasionally for a change of clothing. After I commenced to fly, I occasionally went directly to my apartment from the hangar, taking the plans and the model with me; but I never went out on those nights as I did not dare leave the things in my apartment unguarded.

Danul cooked and served my meals, and Morga Sagra ate with me occasionally. She told me that she had seen Horthal Gyl with Gimmel Gora on several occasions recently, and that Grunge had left his woman and was living in another part of the city. Morga Sagra hadn't seen him for some time now, and she was commencing to feel much safer.

Things seemed to be going along beautifully about this time and then the blow fell—Morga Sagra was arrested.

CHAPTER TEN

INSOFAR AS I WAS concerned, the worst feature of Morga Sagra's arrest was that when they came for her, they found her in my apartment. Of course I didn't have any idea what the charge against her might be; but, if she were suspected of anything, those who associated closely with her would be under suspicion, too.

She was taken away at what would be about seven o'clock in the evening Earth time, and at about ten, Lotar Canl came. He was dressed in the uniform of an officer of the flying force. It was the first time that I had ever seen him in anything but civilian clothes; and I was a little surprised, but I asked no questions.

He came and sat down close to me. "Are you alone?" he asked in a whisper.

"Yes," I said; "I let Danul go out after dinner."

"I have some very bad news for you," he said. "I have just come from the question box in Zabo headquarters. They had Morga Sagra there. That little devil, Horthal Gyl, was there too; it was he who had accused her of being a Unisan spy. A very close friend of mine, in the Zabo, told me that he had also accused you, and he had reported that I was very intimate with you and with Morga Sagra also. They tortured her to make her confess that she was a Unisan spy and that you were also.

"She never admitted that she was anything but a good

Kapar, but in order to save herself from further torture, she told them that you were, just before she died."

"So what?" I asked.

"You have access to a ship whenever you want one. You must escape and that immediately for they will be here for you before midnight."

"But I can't take a ship out unless an officer accompanies me," I said.

"I know that," he replied; "that is the reason for this uniform. I am going with you."

I was instantly suspicious that this might be a trap, for, if I acted on his suggestion and tried to escape, I would be admitting my guilt. I knew that Lotar Canl was an agent of the Zabo, but I had liked him and I had always felt that I could trust him. He saw that I was hesitating.

"You can trust me," he said. "I am not a Kapar."

I looked at him in surprise. "Not a Kapar?" I demanded, "what are you then?"

"The same thing you are, Tangor," he replied—"a Unisan secret agent. I have been here for over ten years, but now that I am under suspicion, my usefulness is at an end. I was advised of your coming and told to look after you. I also knew that Morga Sagra was a traitor. She got what she deserved, but it was a horrible thing to see."

The fact that he knew my name and that he knew that I was an agent and Morga Sagra a traitor convinced me that he had spoken the truth.

"I'll be with you in just a moment," I said; then I got all the plans, drawings, and notes covering the amplifier and burned them, and while they were burning, I smashed the model so that not a single part of it was recognizable.

"Why did you do that?" demanded Lotar Canl.

"I don't want these things to fall into Kapar hands if we are caught," I said; "and I could reproduce that amplifier with my eyes shut; furthermore, there is a perfectly good one on the ship we will fly away."

It was a good thing that I had insisted upon having a fast scout plane, for while we were taxiing up the ramp to take off, an officer shouted at me to return; and then the alarm sounded, rising above the rapid fire of a machine gun, as bullets whistled about us.

Ships shot from half a dozen ramps in pursuit, but they never overtook us.

We flew first to Pud and got a change of clothing and the old Karisan plane from Frink, and then on to Gorvas where my knowledge of Gompth's name came in handy. Lotar Canl showed him his Zabo credentials, and we got a change of clothing and my ship. I had taken the amplifier off the Kapar plane at Pud, and when we reached Orvis, I took it immediately to the Eljanhai, who congratulated me on having so successfully fulfilled a difficult mission.

Just as soon as I could get away from the Eljanhai and the Commissioner for War, I made a beeline for the Harkases. The prospect of seeing them again made me even happier than had the successful fulfillment of my mission. Don and Yamoda were in the garden when I entered, and when Yamoda saw me, she jumped up and ran into the house. Don confronted me with a scowling face.

"Get out!" he growled.

I had been so filled with happiness at the prospect of seeing them, the shock of this greeting stunned me and kept me speechless for a moment, and then my pride prevented me from asking for an explanation. I turned on my heel and left. Blue and despondent, I went back to my old quarters. What had happened? What had I done to deserve such treatment from my best friends? I couldn't understand it, but I had been so terribly hurt that I would not go and ask for an explanation.

I took up my old duties in the flying corps immediately. Never in my life had I flown so recklessly. I invited death on every possible occasion, but I seemed to bear a charmed life; and then, one day, the Eljanhai sent for me.

"Would you like to give the amplifier a serious test?" he asked.

"I certainly would," I replied.

"What do you think would be the best plan?" he asked.

"I will fly to Tonos," I replied.

He did some figuring on a pad of paper and then said, "That will take between thirty-five and forty days. It will be very dangerous. Do you realize the risk?"

"Yes, sir."

"I shall ask for volunteers to go with you," he said.

"I prefer to go alone, sir; there is no use in risking more than one life. I have no ties here. It would not mean anything to anyone, in a personal way, if I never return."

"I thought that you had some very close friends here," he said.

"So did I, but I was mistaken. I'd really prefer to go alone."

"When do you wish to start?" he asked.

"As soon as I can provision my ship; I shall need a great quantity of food and water; much more than enough for a round trip. There's no telling what conditions are like on Tonos. I may not be able to obtain any food or even water there as far as anyone knows."

"Requisition all that you require," he said, "and come and see me again before you take off."

By the following night, I had everything that I needed carefully stowed in my ship, which was equipped with a robot pilot, as were all the great radius ships in Poloda. I could set the robot and sleep all the way to Tonos if I wished; that is, if I could sleep that long.

I was so intrigued with the prospect of this adventure that I was almost happy while I was actively employed, but when I returned to my quarters that last night, possibly and probably my last night on Poloda, my depression returned. I could think of nothing but the reception that Yamoda and Don had given me. My best friends! I tell you, try as I would, I couldn't keep the tears from coming to my eyes as I thought about it.

I was just about ready to peel off my uniform and turn in when there was a knock at my door. "Come in!" I said.

The door opened, and an officer entered. At first I did not recognize him, he had changed so since I had last seen him. It was Handon Gar.

"So you did escape," I said. "I am glad."

He stood for a moment in silence looking at me. "I don't know what to say," he said. "I did you a terrible wrong, and only today did I learn the truth."

"What do you mean?" I asked.

"I thought that you were a traitor, and so reported when I returned to Orvis. When you came back and they didn't arrest you, I was dumbfounded; but I figured that they were giving you more rope with which to hang yourself."

"Then it was you who told Harkas Yamoda?" I asked.

"Yes," he said, "and that was the worst wrong I committed, for I hurt her and Don as much as I did you; but I have been to them and told them the truth. I have just come from them, and they want you to come to their home tonight.

"How did you learn the truth?" I asked.

"The Commissioner for War told me today. He was surprised to know that you had not told anyone."

"I had not received permission; I was still nominally a secret agent."

When I got to the Harkases, none of us could speak for several moments; but finally Don and Yamoda controlled their emotions sufficiently to ask my forgiveness, Yamoda with tears running down her cheeks.

We talked for some time, as they wanted to know all about my experiences in Kapara, and then Don and Handon Gar went into the house, leaving Yamoda and me alone.

We sat in silence for several moments, and then Yamoda said, "Morga Sagra; was she very beautiful?"

"To be perfectly truthful, I couldn't say," I replied. "I suppose she was good-looking enough, but my mind was usually filled with so many other things that I didn't give much thought to Morga Sagra except as a fellow conspirator. I knew she was a traitor, and no traitor could look beautiful to me. Then too I carried with me the memory of someone far more beautiful."

She gave me a quick half-glance, a little questioning look, as though to ask whom that might be; but I didn't have a chance to tell her, for just then Handon Gar and Don came back into the garden and interrupted our conversation.

"What's this I hear of the expedition you're setting out on tomorrow?" demanded Don.

"What expedition?" asked Yamoda.

"He's going to try to fly to Tonos."

"You're joking," said Yamoda.

"Am I, Tangor?" demanded Don.

I shook my head. "He's not joking." Then I told them of the amplifier I had perfected and that the Eljanhai had given me permission to make the flight.

"Not alone, Tangor!" cried Yamoda.

"Yes, alone," I replied.

"Oh, please, if you must go, have somebody with you," she begged; "but must you go?"

"My ship is outfitted, and I leave tomorrow morning," I replied.

Handon Gar begged to go with me. He said that he had permission from the Commissioner for War, if I wished to take him along. Don said he'd like to go, but couldn't as he had another assignment.

"I don't see any reason for risking more than one life," I said, but Yamoda begged me to take Handon Gar along, and he pleaded so eloquently that at last I consented.

That night as I left, I kissed little Yamoda good-bye. It was the first time that we had ever kissed. Until then, she had seemed like a beloved sister to me; now somehow, she seemed different.

Tomorrow Handon Gar and I take off for Tonos, over 570,000 miles away.

Editor's Note: I wonder if Tangor ever reached that little planet winging its way around a strange sun, 450,000 light-years away. I wonder if I shall ever know.

BEYOND THE FARTHEST STAR

BONUS MATERIALS

Bonus material images copyright © Edgar Rice Burroughs, Inc. All rights reserved. Images may not be reproduced without written permission of the publisher.

Bonus Material Contents

Cover of *Blue Book* Magazine, January 1942 . . . 149
Dust Jacket of *Tales of Three Planets* (Collection Featuring First Hardcover Appearance of *Beyond the Farthest Star*), Canaveral Press, 1964 150
Cover of Paperback First Edition, Ace Books, 1964 151
Cover of Paperback Reprint, Ace Books, 1969 152
Cover of Paperback Reprint, Ballantine/Del Rey, 1992 153
Cover of British Paperback, Tandem, 1976. 154
Dust Jacket of *A Soldier of Poloda: Further Adventures Beyond the Farthest Star* by Lee Strong, ERB, Inc., 2017 155
Page from *Beyond the Farthest Star* Comic in *Tarzan*, Vol. 26, No. 218, DC Comics, March 1973 156
Page from *Beyond the Farthest Star* Comic in *Tarzan*, Vol. 26, No. 216, DC Comics, January 1973. 157
Beyond the Farthest Star Online Comic Strip available at ERBurroughs.com 158
Beyond the Farthest Star: Warriors of Zandar #1 Comic Book, American Mythology, July 2021 159
Original Map of the Omos Star System Drawn by Edgar Rice Burroughs 160

Original Map of the Eastern Hemisphere of
   Poloda Drawn by Edgar Rice Burroughs. . 161
Original Map of the Western Hemisphere of
   Poloda Drawn by Edgar Rice Burroughs. . 162
Original Map of the Continent of Unis
   Drawn by Edgar Rice Burroughs 163
Pages from Edgar Rice Burroughs'
   Notebooks 164
First Page of the Original Manuscript of
   Beyond the Farthest Star (Part I) 170
Last Page of the Original Manuscript of
   Beyond the Farthest Star (Part II) with
   Suggested Alternative Titles 171
Letter from Edgar Rice Burroughs to
   Professor J. S. Donaghho,
   November 1, 1940 172
Letter from Professor J. S. Donaghho
   to Edgar Rice Burroughs, with
   ERB's Notes in the Left-hand Margins,
   November 4, 1940 173
Letter from Edgar Rice Burroughs to
   Professor J. S. Donaghho,
   November 7, 1940 175
Letter from Edgar Rice Burroughs to
   Professor J. S. Donaghho,
   November 18, 1940. 176
Letter from Professor J. S. Donaghho
   to Edgar Rice Burroughs, with
   ERB's Note in the Left-hand Margin,
   November 20, 1940. 177
Letter from Edgar Rice Burroughs to
   Professor J. S. Donaghho,
   November 23, 1940. 178

JANUARY 25 CENTS

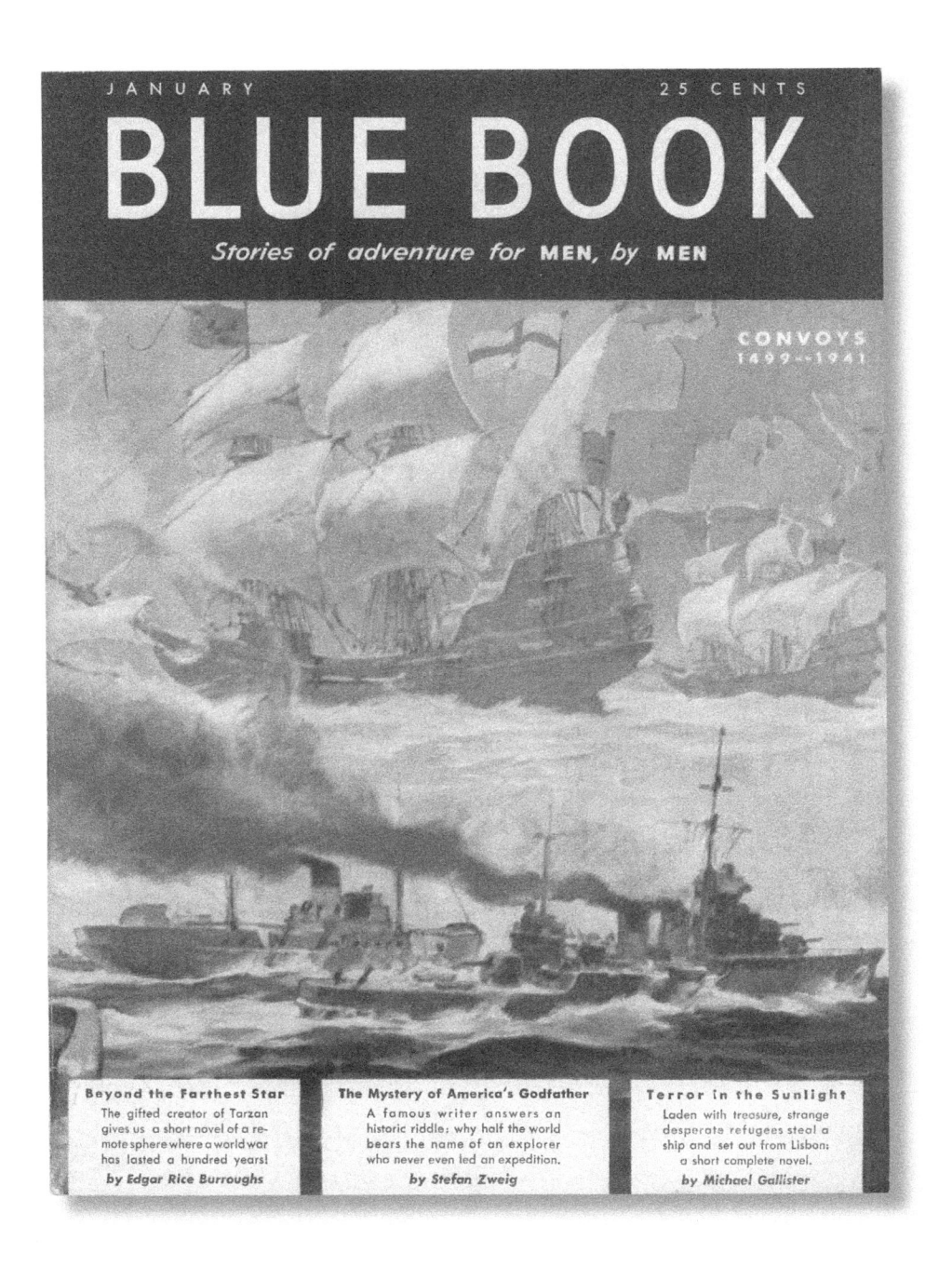

BLUE BOOK

Stories of adventure for **MEN**, *by* **MEN**

CONVOYS
1499–1941

Beyond the Farthest Star
The gifted creator of Tarzan gives us a short novel of a remote sphere where a world war has lasted a hundred years!
by Edgar Rice Burroughs

The Mystery of America's Godfather
A famous writer answers an historic riddle: why half the world bears the name of an explorer who never even led an expedition.
by Stefan Zweig

Terror in the Sunlight
Laden with treasure, strange desperate refugees steal a ship and set out from Lisbon: a short complete novel.
by Michael Gallister

EDGAR
RICE
BURROUGHS

Tales
of
Three
Planets

Tales of Three Planets—

Edgar Rice Burroughs

Canaveral
Press

RGK

ace
SCIENCE
FICTION
CLASSIC
F-282
40¢

EDGAR RICE BURROUGHS

BEYOND THE FARTHEST STAR

A new interplanetary novel by the creator of Tarzan

Complete & Unabridged

ACE | 05654 | $1.25
EDGAR RICE
BURROUGHS
BEYOND THE FARTHEST STAR

EDGAR RICE BURROUGHS

BEYOND THE FARTHEST STAR

Ballantine/37836 (Canada $4.99) U.S. $3.99

Shot down over enemy lines, the man called Tangor had lived to fight again on a far, distant world!

Edgar Rice Burroughs
Beyond the Farthest Star

A Soldier of Poloda

The Wild Adventures of Edgar Rice Burroughs® Series 5

Further Adventures Beyond The Farthest Star

Lee Strong

SOMEWHERE IN THE ENDLESS VOID OF TIME AND SPACE, LT. R. FARNSWORTH OF THE *R.A.F.* FINDS HIMSELF A *CASTAWAY* -- MAROONED ON AN ALIEN WORLD -- AMONGST THE STRANGE INHABITANTS OF A PLACE BEYOND ANY MORTAL MAN'S IMAGINATION!

PRINCESS of DOOM!

SO... THAT'S YOUR *FAMILY*, EH? I WISH YOU COULD TELL ME IF THEIR EXPRESSIONS ARE *FRIENDLY* OR NOT!

SPRRT... GRRP!

NOW CALLED *TANGOR*, HE FOLLOWS A SMALL SIMIAN-LIKE CREATURE WHOM HE HAS BEFRIENDED...

beyond the farthest star

CAN'T FIGHT BACK...THIS SHIP ISN'T ARMED!
I'VE GOT TO OUTRUN 'EM...INTO OUTER SPACE!
CANNOT MAINTAIN ORBIT... WILL MAKE THIS TEST THE REAL THING!
I'M BEYOND THEIR RANGE NOW... BUT--THE SHIP'S BEEN HIT!
CAN'T... MANEUVER HER! CONTROLS ARE JAMMED!
HOURS SEEM TO STRETCH INTO CENTURIES...UNTIL-
I'M HEADING FOR A SMALL PLANETOID! THE SHIP'S CAUGHT IN ITS GRAVITATIONAL FIELD...
IT-IT'S *GASP* GETTING HARD TO... BREATHE...
GASP MY GILLS... AREN'T... FUNCTIONING! *GASP*
4

158

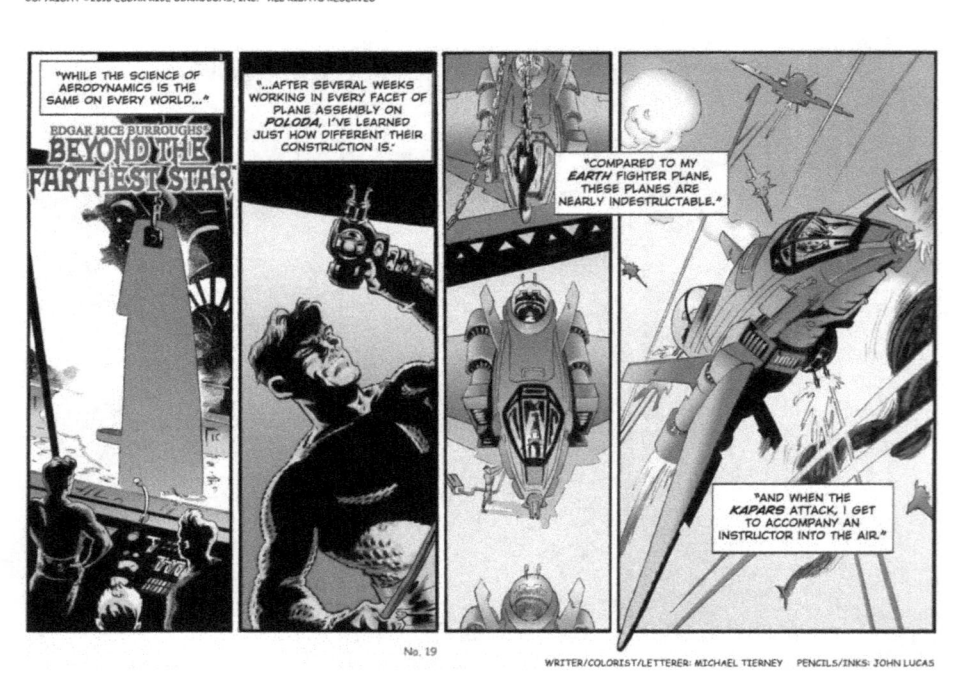

EDGAR RICE BURROUGHS UNIVERSE™
BEYOND THE
FARTHEST STAR™
WARRIORS OF ZANDAR
MAIN EDITION
1 US 3.99
FOUR-ISSUE MINI-SERIES
AMERICAN MYTHOLOGY PRODUCTIONS
OFFICIAL
ERB
UNIVERSE
CANON
BEEZZZ STUDIO

Diagram of the Planetary System

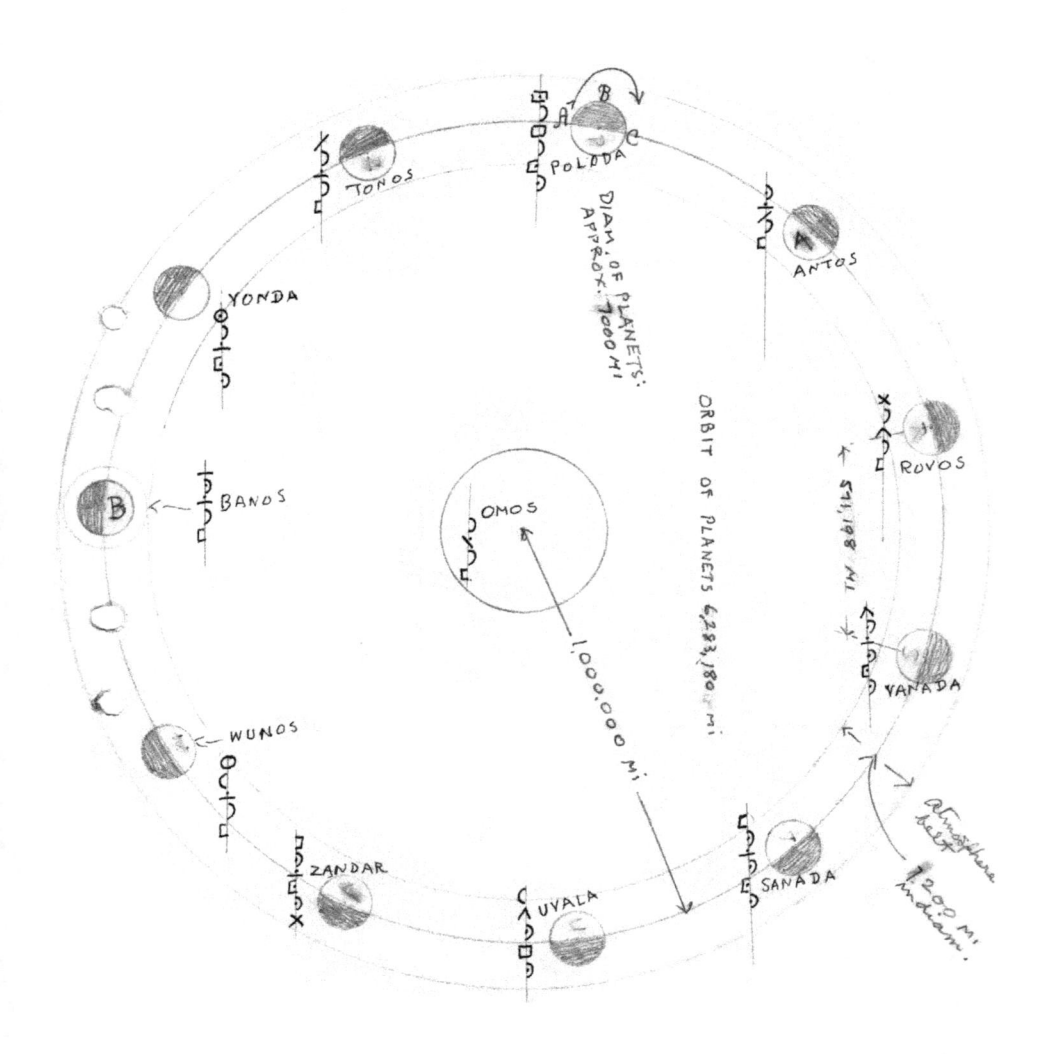

- **POLODA** (with A, B, C markers)
- **TONOS**
- **YONDA**
- **BANDS** (B)
- **WUNOS**
- **ZANDAR**
- **UVALA** (C)
- **SANADA** (E)
- **VANADA**
- **ROVOS**
- **ANTOS** (A)
- **OMOS** (center)

DIAM. OF PLANETS: APPROX. 7000 MI

ORBIT OF PLANETS 6,293,180 MI

1,000,000 MI

1M 801,115

atmosphere belt 1,200 MI in diam.

Eastern
Hemisphere

MAP of UNIS

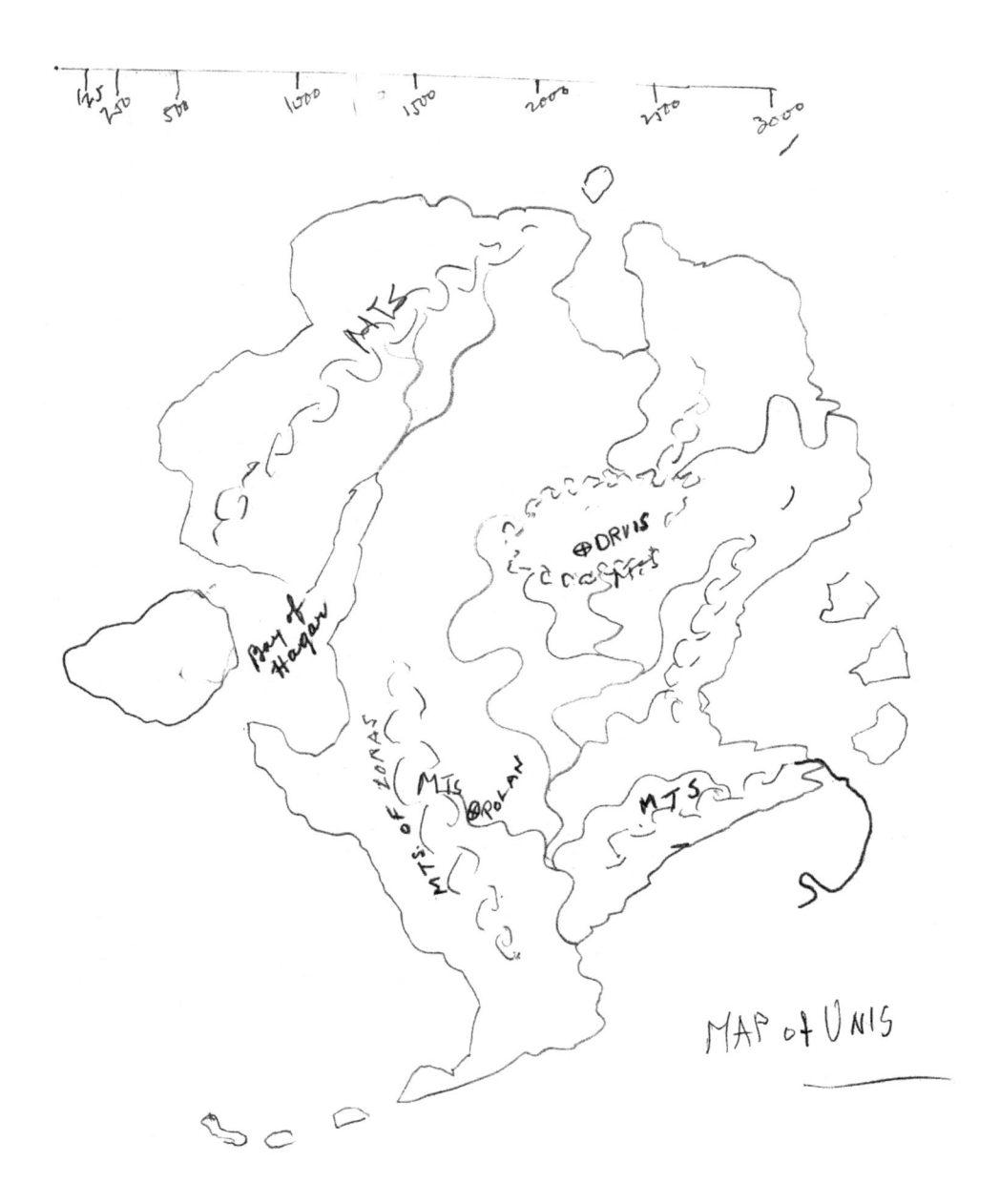

UNISAN ALPHABET WITH ENGLISH EQUIVALENTS

	usa	u		luh	l
	om	o		pan	p
	eta	e		tam	t
	ava	a		fuh	f
	ila	i		ju	j
	wuh	w		mi	m
	yak	y		ruh	r
	bos	b		vik	v
	gar	g		sha	ch
	kob	k		ang	ng
	nuh	n		There is no c, q, or x	
	sko	s		comma	
	zuh	z		period	
	dar	d		interrogation	
	hul	h			

On the planet of Poloda five continents there are
ara li tovos thu Poloda tan pandarvan huvo tu

0	dot	⊥
1	al	∣
2	van	P
3	soo	⊥
4	Lo	V
5	tan	φ
6	huv	Φ
7	jan	Ⅱ
8	bor	Ⅺ
9	ko	Ⅲ
10	aldot	
11	alal	
12	alvan	
13	alsoo	
20	vandot	
21	vandotal	
22	vandotvan	
30	soodot	
40	dodot	
50	tandot	
100	aldotdot	

```
1298 Kapiolani Boulevard                                              LXXXVIII-1
Honolulu  T H
                    BEYOND THE FARTHEST STAR
                      by Edgar Rice Burroughs                Words: 21,574
                    Commenced:   Oct 24 1940                 Chaps: 13
                    Finished:    Nov 5 1940                  Pages: 63
            (From Oct 24 to Oct 30 I wrote Escape on Mars)
   Globular Cluster N.G.C. 7006 - 220,000 lt yrs. Jeans pg 61
 2 Harkas Yen - the psychiatrist
   Poloda - the planet P
   Kapars - the enemies
   Tangor (from nothing) name given to narrator
   Unis - the country and continent
   tan - from
   gor - nothing
   Harkas Don - Harkas Yen's son
   Harkas Yamoda - Harkas Yen's daughter
   Orvis - the city
   Canapa - Unis name for Globular Cluster NGC 7006
   Balzo Maro - the girl who discovered Tangor
   COSTUMES:  Girls (adult single) gold with red boots
              Police - red with black boots
              Harkas Yen - black with white boots
              Judges - gray with gray boots
              Soldiers - blue, blue boots, blue helmets
              Labor Corps - dark brown with dark brown boots
              Ordinary working clothes (all classes, both sexes) ecru
                 with ecru boots
              Married women - silver with silver boots
              Widows - purple with purple boots
              Little girls - all pink
              Little boys - all yellow
       HAIR:  Girls, copper titian; men, blond
 3 Janhai - the commission (7 elected) rulers of Unis
   jan - 7
   hai - elect
   Eljanhai - highest commissioner (President)
   el - highest
   Omos - the Polodian sun
   THE JANHAI: Commissioners for WAR: FOREIGN (STATE): COMMERCE:
               INTERIOR: EDUCATION: TREASURY: JUSTICE
   Unisans - the people of Unis
 5 Kapara - country of the Kapars
 7 Bay of Hagar - on west coast of Unis
   Bantor Han - surviving gunner on Tangor's ship
   Polan - city in southern Unis
   Mountains of Loras -  "       "
 8 lion of Poloda - similar to African lion, but striped like zebra
10 Epris - a continent on Poloda
   Ergos - capital of Kapara
   Karagan Ocean
   Karis - a continent on Poloda
   Punos - country on Epris, subjugated by Kapars
   Balzo Jan - brother of Balzo Maro
12 Island of Despair - off southern tip of Unis
13 Uvala - the planet U
```

```
Chapters
  F -  1
  1 -, 2
  2 -  6
  3 - 11
  4 - 14
  5 - 17
  6 - 22
  7 - 28
  8 - 32
  9 - 36
 10 - 41
 11 - 46
 12 - 52
 13 - 58
END - 63
```

WORD COUNT

```
pg   wds   lns
14   345   29
15   340   31
16   317   31
17   324   29
18   371   31
19   346   31
 6  2043  182
```

wds per line - 11.225
wds per pg   - 347.975 (31 lns to pg)

```
63 pgs @ 347.975    -   21,922
Less 7 lns pg 1
     24 lns chp hds
     31 lns @ 11.225 -      348
          TOTAL WORDS     21,574
```

1298 Kapiolani Boulevard
Honolulu

TANGOR RETURNS
by Edgar Rice Burroughs
Commenced: Dec 17 1940
Finished: Dec 21 1940

Words: 20,695
Chaps: 10
Pages: 58

1. Morga Sagra - girl traitor
   Handon Gar - Unisan officer, prisoner in Kapara
   Tonos - a planet
   Antos - a planet
   Gorvas - a city in Karis
   Gompth - a Kapar agent in Gorvas
   Pud - a city in Auris
   Auris - a continent on Poloda
   Frink - Kapar agent in Pud
   Gurrul - head of Kapar secret police
   Zabo - the secret police of Kapar
   Tunzo Bor - Unisan prisoner in Kapara
   Pom Da (Great I) head of Kapars
   Gimmel Gora - a woman
   Grunge - her male companion
   Korvan Don - name assumed by Tangor for use in Kapara
   Lotar Canl - Tangor's manservant in Ergos
   Horthal Wend - a Kapar
   Haka Gera - his woman
   Horthal Gyl - their son
2. Voldan Ocean
   Mandan Ocean
3. 267M9436 - Tangor's prison number in Kapara
5. Highest Most High - mode of address for the Pom Da
8. Danul - Tangor's 2nd man servant in Ergos

WORD COUNT:

9 pgs = 3328 wds and 280 lns; an average of 11.88 wds per line.
1742 lns (actual count) at 11.88 wds per ln = 20,695 wds.

If these 3 or 4 novelettes are ever published in book form, combine them as Book One, Book Two, etc., using all the Forewords.

LXXXVIII-I

Distance Earth to Poloda   450,000 lt yrs Earth time
                           548,000   Poloda time
TIME: Usa (day of wk) 2 (month) 15,321 (yr)
      Recorded history ante dates yr 1 5000 yrs
      Beyond this is largely legend
      300 days to year
       30 days to month
       10 days to week
      Months are numbered 1 to 10
      Days of week are named for the first ten letters in Unis
      alphabet: Usa, Om, Eta, Ava, Ila, Wuh, Yak, Bos, Gar, Kob.
ALPHABET: (with English equivalent) usa-u;om-o;eta-e; ava-a;ila-i;
      wuh-w; yak-y; bos-b; gar-g; kob-k; nuh-n; sko-s; zuh-z; dar-d;
      hul-h; luh-l; pan-p; tam-t; fuh-f; ju-j; mi-m; ruh-r; vik-v;
      sha-ch(as in church); ang-ng(as in thing) no c, q, or x
POPULATION OF UNIS: 130,000,000; about 16,000,000 adult women, bear-
      ing 10,000,000 children a year, over half of which are boys,
      of whom some 5,000,000 grow to maturity.
PLANE PRODUCTION: 40 plants with ten assembly lines in each, each
      line turning out 1 plane per hour for a 10 hr day during 27
      working days per month - 270 planes per mo. per assembly line;
      2700 per month per plant, 108,000 per month for 40 plants.
      10 plants turn out heavy bombers
      10   light bombers
      10   combat planes
      10   pursuit or recomnaisance planes

Honolulu

BEYOND THE FARTHEST STAR
by Edgar Rice Burroughs

THIS STORY, SUBMITTED FOR FIRST U.S. AND CANADIAN MAGAZINE RIGHTS ONLY, TO BE COPYRIGHTED IN THE NAME OF EDGAR RICE BURROUGHS

Foreword

We had attended a party at Diamond Head; and after dinner, comfortable on hikiee and easy chair on the lanai, we fell to talking about the legends and superstitions of the ancient Hawaiians.

There were a number of old timers there, several with a mixture of Hawaiian and American blood, and we were the only malihinis - happy to be there, and happy to listen.

Most Hawaiian legends are rather childish, though often amusing; but many of their superstitions are grim and sinister - and they are not confined to ancient Hawaiians either. You couldn't get a modern kane or wahine with a drop of Hawaiian blood in their veins to touch the bones or relics still often found in hidden burial caves in the mountains, nor many haole kamaainas either, for that matter. They seem to feel the same way about kahunas, and that it is just as easy to be polite to a kahuna as not - and much safer.

I am not superstitious, and I don't believe in ghosts; so what I heard that evening didn't have any other effect on me than to entertain me. It couldn't have been connected in any way with what happened later that night, for I scarcely gave it a thought after we left the home of our friends; and I really don't know why I have mentioned it at all, except that it has to do with strange happenings; and what happened later that night certainly falls into that categOry.

We had come home quite early; and I was in bed by eleven o'clock, but I couldn't sleep; so I got up about midnight, thinking I would work a little on the outline of a new story I had in mind.

170

Listen! The sirens are sounding the general alarm.

Editor's Note: I have sat before my typewriter at midnight many a night since that last line was typed by unseen hands. I have wondered if Tangor ever came back from the battle to which that general alarm called him, or if he died a second death. I am still wondering.

                    THE END

Note: Suggested alternative titles:
                    IT IS WAR
                    THE GHOSTLY SCRIPT

1298 Kapiolani Boulevard
Honolulu

November 1 1940

Professor J. S. Donaghho,
913 Alewa Drive, Honolulu.

My dear Professor Donaghho:

I asked my friend, Dr. Livesay, if he would suggest an authority on astronomy whom I might approach for a little assistance in a very weighty astrnomical problem which confronts me; and he very kindly gave me your name.

Accordingly, I telephoned you today but received no answer; so I am taking the liberty of writing you instead.

The problem is in relation to one of those very profound classics which I have been inflicting on a very tolerant world for a quarter of a century.

The enclosed pencil sketch is a diagram of an imaginary solar system consisting of a small sun and eleven equally spaced planets. An atmosphere belt rotates about the sun at the same speed as the planets.

Following, are some of the questions I would like to ask:

    1. Could the planets describe a circle in their orbits, or must it be an elipse?

    2. Assuming that we are living on planet P, what planets would be visible to us at night; and what planets, if any, would be visible by day?

    3. What effect would the sun and the other planets have on the ocean tides on any of the planets, assuming that the oceans are as large as those on Earth? What I wished to determine was whether the tides would be so terrific as to preclude all forms of ocean navigation.

    4. If there were a sphere eight thousand miles in diameter, composed entirely of atmosphere of the same density as our atmosphere at sea level, and this sphere was at the same distance from the sun as is the Earth, would it reflect the sun's light so as to be visible from any of the planets at night?

I shall greatly appreciate any help you can give me, and I apologize for inflicting anything like this on you.

                  Very sincerely yours,

Q = A
X = B

913 Alewa Drive, Honolulu, T. H.
November 4, 1940

Mr. Edgar Rice Burroughs
1298 Kapiolani Blvd.
Honolulu.

My dear Mr. Burroughs:
Yours of November 1 reached me this afternoon. As there are only two of us in Honolulu (as it seems) who have more than a modicum of astronomical information, it is probably natural that our reputation in that direction is somewhat exaggerated -- as we answer the occasional qestions turned over to us by the newspapers. I take great pleasure in giving you what I believe to be perfectly accurate answers to your questions.

1. Any planet could revolve around the sun in a circle, if it had a certain velocity, of a value depending upon the combined mass of the sun and the planet. As a result, the required velocity for two planets of different mass would not be the same, so your planets must all have exactly the same mass, or they will not remain equally spaced. [a certain point]   [a given]

2. If planet P rotates in the direction, of my crude arrow, an observer at A would see planet V a little above the setting sun, and W, X, Y, Z each higher up, Z near the zenith. V would set first, then W, X, Y and Z in succession, Z about midnight, when the planet has carried the observer to B. Then Q would rise, and R, S, T and U in succession, the last just before sunrise. Thus, if his job kept him up all night, and the weather was clear, our observer would have a chance to see all of the planets in one night. (Anyone could see all the stars visible in his [north] latitude, by staying out all night, on a perfectly clear night between October 1 and March 1).
Such a positive answer cannot be given as to visibility in the daytime. At her greatest brilliancy, Venus may be visible most of a clear day, as she is then at less than half her usual distance from the earth. From analogy we may infer that possibly Q and Z might be visible in the daytime. Probably none of the others, with the doubtful exception of R and Y.

3. The tidal efficiency of the sun varies inversely as the cube of the distance. So, at a distance of 1,000,000 miles, its efficiency would be about 800,000 times as great as at this distance. So the tides would not only preclude all forms of ocean navigation, but would, in all likelihood, sweep daily over the whole of the continents, thus precluding all forms of life!

4. Such a sphere, if it could exist, would not be visible at all if cloudless. If filled with clouds, it would be visible, but to what distance would be very difficult to determine. However, gases will not retain spherical form, unless contained in spherical vessels, or held by gravitational attraction, as in the case of the earth and Mars. As the attraction of Mars for bodies on its surface is about two-fifths that of the earth, the atmosphere of Mars is much less dense than that of the earth -- that is, if it ever had more atmosphere, the gases have escaped into space. As the moon's surface at-

traction is only one-sixth that of the earth, she has no atmosphere at all -- if she ever had any it has escaped into space, entirely.

5. Now, I hope that your atmospheric belt is not an essential part of the plan, as I must assure you that it would not "stay put". If the planets did not have as much atmosphere as they could hold (a fairly definite amount), each one would draw in from the surrounding belt enough to fill out its quota, and the rest would be diffused in all directions. Some part of the total would be taken up by the sun, if it did not have its full quota, and the rest would be diffused throughout space.

No apology necessary for "inflicting anything like this" on me, as this has been fun!!! If I can be of any more assistance, please do not hesitate to let me know. I should be glad to answer by mail again, or give you an interview, if you should prefer.

Very truly yours,

J. S. Donaghho

N. B. -- As I am now my own secretary, there will be an embarrassing number of interlineations in this. Please pardon!

1298 Kapiolani Boulevard
Honolulu

November 7 1940

Professor J S Donaghho,
913 Alewa Drive, Honolulu.

My dear Professor Donaghho:

I cannot tell you how much I appreciated your courtesy and generosity in giving me so much of your time and the very interesting and helpful replies to my questions.

The total loss of the atmosphere band desolated me, especially inasmuch as I had already used it in the first installment of the story. In the next installment, I shall alibi myself out of it with as much ease as was displayed by the daring young man on the flying trapeze.

Again thanking you, and trusting that I may have the pleasure of meeting you some day, I am,

Very cordially yours,

Dr Donghho's letter filed with notes on "Beyond the Farthest Star" or "Ghostly Script"

xxxxxxxxxxxx
1298 Kapiolani Blvd.
Honolulu, Hawaii

November 18, 1940

Professor J. S. Donaghho
913 Alewa Drive
Honolulu, Hawaii

My dear Professor Donaghho:

       In studying your letter of November 4th, another inquiry occurs to me.

       In paragraph 3, in discussing the tides, I cannot tell whether you based your deductions on the assumption that my imaginary sun was of the same size as our own sun, or not. It is supposed to be very much smaller, just large enough to give forth enough heat to maintain a rather springlike temperature on the planets, which are one million miles distant.

       I thought that this smaller sun might not produce tides that would preclude all forms of ocean navigation, and I also wondered what effect the pull of the other planets would have on the tides. The nearest of these planets to Planet P is a little over half a million miles, and there is one of these at this distance on either side of the Planet P.

       If this bores you, pay no attention to it, but you said, perhaps unwisely, that you found it fun.

       Again thanking you for your kindness, and with best wishes, I am

       Very sincerely yours,

ERB:P

913 Alewa Drive, Honolulu, T. H.
November 20, 1940.

Mr. Edgar Rice Burroughs
1298 Kapiolani Blvd
Honolulu, T. H.

My dear Mr. Burroughs:

Replying to yours of November 18:

My rather startling conclusion as to the tides on your imaginary planets was based upon the assumption that your sun was of the same mass as ours, and your planets of the same mass as the earth. Tidal efficiency depends upon the product of the masses, and the cube of the distance.

If the mean density of your sun were the same as that of our sun, and its diameter about 20 % greater than that of the earth, on a planet whose mass was the same as our earth, and at a distance of one million miles, it would raise tides about the same as ours.

Planets of the same mass as the earth, and distant from each other about 500,000 miles, would tend to raise tides in each other almost twice as great as ours. However, since, in your system, the two nearest any planet are almost opposite each other, their tidal effects upon that planet would almost neutralize each other. Each of the next pair would tend to raise tides about one-fourth as great as ours, and their effects would not so nearly neutralize each other. In fact, The tidal effects of the planets would probably be to slightly reduce (split infinitive?) the effect of the sun. As a result, to produce tides equal to ours, the diameter of your sun might have to be some 25 % greater than that of the earth.

You were certainly assured that I would take pleasure in answering any further questions, if I could do so, and the assurance is again extended to you. This has b en fun!

Very truly yours

J. S. Donaghho

1298 Kapiolani Boulevard
Honolulu

November 23 1940

Professor J. S. Donaghho,
913 Alewa Drive, Honolulu.

My dear Professor Donaghho:

Once more, thanks for your kind assistance, which has been most helpful. You have proven yourself a real benefactor to the human race on Poloda (Planet P) by lowering the tides so as to permit ocean navigation.

In the little matter of the atmosphere belt, there are two schools of thought on Poloda: One adheres to the Donaghhoan theory, while the other, hopefully anticipating inter-planetary navigation, clings stubbornly to the Burroughsian theory.

I am glad that you found fun in answering my queries. I find fun in the imaginings which prompt them; and I can appreciate, in a small way, the swell time God had in creating the Universe.

Again thanking you, and with kindest regards, believe me,

                Very sincerely yours,

Edgar Rice Burroughs: Master of Adventure

The creator of the immortal characters Tarzan of the Apes and John Carter of Mars, EDGAR RICE BURROUGHS is one of the world's most popular authors. Mr. Burroughs' timeless tales of heroes and heroines transport readers from the jungles of Africa and the dead sea bottoms of Barsoom to the miles-high forests of Amtor and the savage inner world of Pellucidar, and even to alien civilizations beyond the farthest star. Mr. Burroughs' books are estimated to have sold hundreds of millions of copies, and they have spawned 60 films and 250 television episodes.

About the Cover Artist

FRANK FRAZETTA (1928–2010) was an American artist of fantasy, science fiction, and popular culture. He is often regarded as the "Godfather" of fantasy art, and is one of the most renowned illustrators of the twentieth century. Throughout the 1960s and 1970s, his artwork graced the covers of dozens of Edgar Rice Burroughs' books.

About the Frontispiece Artist

MARK SCHULTZ is an American cartoonist, illustrator, and author whose interest in adventure fiction and the sciences led him to create his award-winning *Xenozoic Tales* comics, as well as *SubHuman*, in collaboration with paleontologist Dr. Michael J. Ryan. He has illustrated a collection of Robert E. Howard's Conan of Cimmeria and written the science primer *The Stuff of Life: A Graphic Guide to Genetics and DNA*. His illustrated novella, *Storms at Sea*, was released in 2015. Currently, he writes the adventures of Prince Valiant for King Features Syndicate and is in the process of creating a new *Xenozoic* story. His illustrations, commissions, and sketches can be found collected in the *Carbon* series.

About the Illustrator

ROY G. KRENKEL (1918–1983) was a noted American science fiction and fantasy artist who was a mentor to the legendary Frank Frazetta. Danton Burroughs said of him, "Roy Krenkel was a key factor in the 1960s revival of my grandfather's writings. Krenkel's illustrations forever secured his position as one of the all-time great Edgar Rice Burroughs illustrators."

About Edgar Rice Burroughs, Inc.

Founded in 1923 by Edgar Rice Burroughs, one of the first authors to incorporate himself, EDGAR RICE BURROUGHS, INC., holds numerous trademarks and the rights to all literary works of the author still protected by copyright, including stories of Tarzan of the Apes and John Carter of Mars. The company oversees authorized adaptations of his literary works in film, television, radio, publishing, theatrical stage productions, licensing, and merchandising. Edgar Rice Burroughs, Inc., continues to manage and license the vast archive of Mr. Burroughs' literary works, fictional characters, and corresponding artworks that has grown for over a century. The company is still owned by the Burroughs family and remains headquartered in Tarzana, California, the town named after the Tarzana Ranch Mr. Burroughs purchased there in 1919 that led to the town's future development.

In 2015, under the leadership of President James Sullos, the company relaunched its publishing division, which was founded by Mr. Burroughs in 1931. With the publication of new authorized editions of Mr. Burroughs' works and brand-new novels and stories by today's talented authors, the company continues its long tradition of bringing tales of wonder and imagination featuring the Master of Adventure's many iconic characters and exotic worlds to an eager reading public.

Visit **EdgarRiceBurroughs.com** for more information.

JOIN EDGAR RICE BURROUGHS FANDOM!

The Burroughs Bibliophiles

The only fan organization to be personally approved by Edgar Rice Burroughs, The Burroughs Bibliophiles is the largest ERB fan club in the world, with members spanning the globe and maintaining local chapters across the United States and in England.

Also endorsed by Burroughs, *The Burroughs Bulletin*, the organization's official publication, features fascinating articles, essays, interviews, and more centered on the rich history and continuing legacy of the Master of Adventure. The Bibliophiles also annually sponsors the premier ERB fan convention.

Regular membership dues include:

- *Four issues of* The Burroughs Bulletin
- *The Gridley Wave newsletter in PDF*
- *The latest news in ERB fandom*
- *Information about the annual ERB fan convention*

For more information about the society and membership, visit BurroughsBibliophiles.com or The Burroughs Bibliophiles Facebook page, or email the Editor at BurroughsBibliophiles@gmail.com.

Call (573) 647-0225
or mail
318 Patriot Way,
Yorktown, Virginia
23693-4639, USA.

Trademarks Edgar Rice Burroughs® and Tarzan® owned by Edgar Rice Burroughs, Inc. and used by permission.

JOIN AMERICAN MYTHOLOGY PRODUCTIONS AS WE EMBARK ON AN INCREDIBLE JOURNEY
BEYOND THE
FARTHEST STAR™
ERB INC.™
AMERICAN MYTHOLOGY PRODUCTIONS™
AN ALL-NEW CANONICAL COMIC BOOK SERIES BY MIKE WOLFER & ALESSANDRO RANALDI ON SALE NOW!
OFFICIAL ERB UNIVERSE™ CANON
SHOP OUR ENTIRE LIBRARY OF ERB TITLES AT AMERICANMYTHOLOGY.NET!

EDGAR RICE BURROUGHS AUTHORIZED LIBRARY™

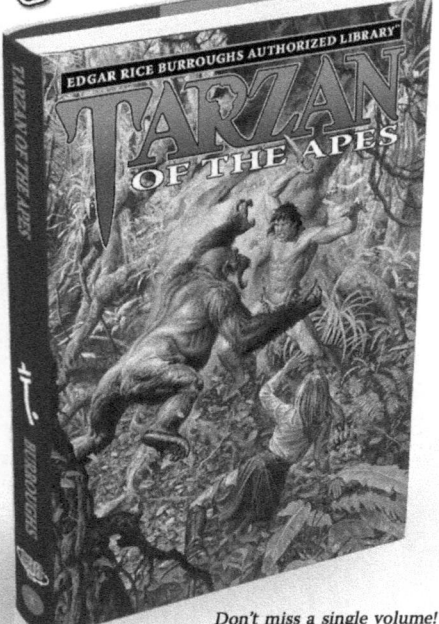

COLLECT EVERY VOLUME!

For the first time ever, the Edgar Rice Burroughs Authorized Library presents the complete literary works of the Master of Adventure in handsome uniform editions. Published by the company founded by Burroughs himself in 1923, each volume of the Authorized Library is packed with extras and rarities not to be found in any other edition. From cover art and frontispieces by legendary artist Joe Jusko to forewords and afterwords by today's authorities and luminaries to a treasure trove of bonus materials mined from the company's extensive archives in Tarzana, California, the Edgar Rice Burroughs Authorized Library will take you on a journey of wonder and imagination you will never forget.

Don't miss a single volume! Sign up for email updates at ERBurroughs.com to keep apprised of all 80-plus editions of the Authorized Library as they become available.

1. TARZAN OF THE APES
2. THE RETURN OF TARZAN
3. THE BEASTS OF TARZAN
4. THE SON OF TARZAN
5. TARZAN AND THE JEWELS OF OPAR
6. JUNGLE TALES OF TARZAN
7. TARZAN THE UNTAMED
8. TARZAN THE TERRIBLE
9. TARZAN AND THE GOLDEN LION
10. TARZAN AND THE ANT MEN
11. TARZAN, LORD OF THE JUNGLE
12. TARZAN AND THE LOST EMPIRE
13. TARZAN AT THE EARTH'S CORE
14. TARZAN THE INVINCIBLE
15. TARZAN TRIUMPHANT
16. TARZAN AND THE CITY OF GOLD
17. TARZAN AND THE LION MEN
18. TARZAN AND THE LEOPARD MEN
19. TARZAN'S QUEST
20. TARZAN THE MAGNIFICENT
21. TARZAN AND THE FORBIDDEN CITY
22. TARZAN AND THE FOREIGN LEGION
23. TARZAN AND THE MADMAN
24. TARZAN AND THE CASTAWAYS

THE JOURNEY BEGINS AT ERBURROUGHS.COM

ERB INC.™

© Edgar Rice Burroughs, Inc. All rights reserved. Edgar Rice Burroughs®, Edgar Rice Burroughs Authorized Library™, Tarzan®, and Tarzan of the Apes™ owned by Edgar Rice Burroughs, Inc. The Doodad symbol and all logos are trademarks of Edgar Rice Burroughs, Inc.

THE SWORDS OF ETERNITY™ SUPER-ARC CONTINUES!

A NEW CANONICAL JOHN CARTER® OF MARS® NOVEL BY GEARY GRAVEL

INCLUDES THE BONUS NOVELETTE STORMWINDS OF VA-NAH™ STARRING VICTORY HARBEN™ IN THE WORLD OF THE MOON MAID™ BY ANN TONSOR ZEDDIES

EDGAR RICE BURROUGHS UNIVERSE™
JOHN CARTER® OF MARS®
GODS OF THE FORGOTTEN
GEARY GRAVEL

ALSO AVAILABLE:
CARSON OF VENUS®: THE EDGE OF ALL WORLDS BY MATT BETTS
&
TARZAN®: BATTLE FOR PELLUCIDAR® BY WIN SCOTT ECKERT

ERB INC.

AVAILABLE NOW AT ERBURROUGHS.COM

Copyright © Edgar Rice Burroughs, Inc. All rights reserved. Trademarks Edgar Rice Burroughs®, Edgar Rice Burroughs Universe™, John Carter®, John Carter of Mars®, Victory Harben™, The Moon Maid™, Va-nah™, Carson of Venus®, Tarzan®, Pellucidar®, and Swords of Eternity™ owned by Edgar Rice Burroughs, Inc. Associated logos are trademarks or registered trademarks of Edgar Rice Burroughs, Inc.

THE WILD ADVENTURES OF EDGAR RICE BURROUGHS™

Tarzan: Return to Pal-ul-don by Will Murray

Tarzan on the Precipice a novel by Michael A. Sanford

Tarzan Trilogy Thomas Zachek

Tarzan: The Greystoke Legacy Under Siege

A Soldier of Poloda: Further Adventures Beyond The Farthest Star Lee Strong

Swords Against the Moon Men Christopher Paul Carey

Untamed Pellucidar Lee Strong

Tarzan and the Revolution Thomas Zachek

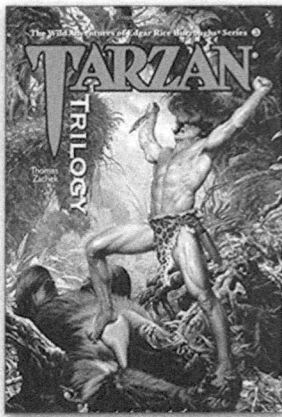

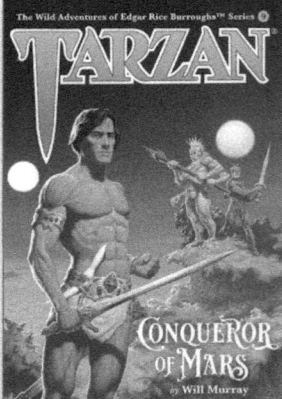

Tarzan: Conqueror of Mars by Will Murray

NEW NOVELS OF TRULY WILD ADVENTURE, EVEN MOVING BEYOND CLASSIC CANON!

AVAILABLE NOW AT ERBURROUGHS.COM

ERB INC.™

© Edgar Rice Burroughs, Inc. All rights reserved. Trademarks including Edgar Rice Burroughs®, Tarzan®, Pellucidar®, The Moon Men™, Beyond the Farthest Star™, and The Wild Adventures of Edgar Rice Burroughs™ owned by Edgar Rice Burroughs, Inc.

Edgar Rice Burroughs, Inc.

A whole universe of ERB collectibles, including books, T-shirts, DVDs, statues, puzzles, playing cards, dust jackets, art prints, and MORE!

Your one-stop destination for all things ERB!

ERB INC.

VISIT US ONLINE AT ERBurroughs.com

© Edgar Rice Burroughs, Inc. All rights reserved. Trademarks Edgar Rice Burroughs®, Edgar Rice Burroughs Universe™, Tarzan®, Dejah Thoris®, John Carter®, and Warlord of Mars® owned by Edgar Rice Burroughs, Inc.

Lightning Source UK Ltd.
Milton Keynes UK
UKHW012135050922
408396UK00007B/159/J